1/26

CW01630640

A Man and a Mountain

Robert Longhurst

Copyright © 2025 Robert Longhurst

All rights reserved.

No part of this book may be copied, stored in an electronic retrieval system, photocopied, tweeted, TikToked, set to music, or adapted into a musical or a Netflix limited series without the prior written permission of the author. (If you *are* planning a musical, at least let me play a tree in the background).

This is a work of fiction, based on true events. Which is a polite way of saying: yes, I really did climb that mountain on Christmas Day; yes, there really was a man with biscuits; and yes, it was as cold and miserable as described. But the rest has been adapted, altered, or completely imagined – partly for dramatic purposes and partly to protect the innocent, the guilty, and anyone with a good lawyer.

Any resemblance to actual persons, living or dead, beyond those inspirations, is purely coincidental apart from the bits that aren't. If you think you recognise yourself, don't worry. You're probably mistaken. And if you're not mistaken – well, congratulations, you made it into a book.

If you've read this far into the copyright page, you probably deserve a custard cream.

Published in the United Kingdom.

First edition.

SNAILWHISPER
PRESS

Snailwhisper Press
ISBN: 978-1-0682234-3-3

For my mum

For always keeping a seat at your table,
no matter how late I arrive,
how lost I've been,
or how many times I've said I wasn't coming.

This book is for you
because you have always kept a seat for me.

Skip the second epilogue; you'll prefer the ending you imagined.

CONTENT NOTE

This story explores themes of grief, depression, and suicide. If those subjects are difficult for you, please take care while reading.

If you are struggling, you are not alone.
Support is available:

In the UK, you can call Samaritans on 116 123 at any time.

In the US, you can call or text 988 for the 988 Suicide & Crisis Lifeline.

Elsewhere, please check local helplines or speak to someone you trust.

Stories can be heavy, but they can also carry hope.
I hope you find some here.

Grief will walk beside you up every path.
Hope waits quietly at the summit.

– Yusuf

PROLOGUE
THE MOUNTAIN

The mountain was waiting.

It had waited through storms and summers, through the boot prints of strangers, and through the stillness of years when no one came.

It waited without hurry, without need.

Snow fell, thawed, and fell again. Stones shifted under the patience of time. Streams carved new lines into its skin. Moss crept, frost retreated, and clouds passed like brief thoughts across its brow, and still the mountain remained – patient, ancient, unmoved.

It had listened to laughter once, and to the ragged curses of those who found its slopes less forgiving than they'd imagined.

It had heard songs, sobs, and prayers lost to the gale.

It had felt the thud of boots and the rhythm of hearts.

It had tasted blood and rain and kept both without distinction.

It had known the lightness of triumph and the heaviness of grief.

People carried their stories up its paths.

Some came seeking challenge.

Some came chasing beauty.

Some came hoping to leave something behind.

The mountain never promised answers. It only listened, as it always had and always would.

It watched centuries pass in quiet patience. Whole generations were born, loved, and gone again, their voices now part of the wind that whispered across its stones.

The mountain did not mourn.

It simply remained.

Seasons folded over it like pages of an endless book – each snow, each thaw, another sentence in a story that had no need of an ending.

And still, it waited.

On Christmas morning, it listened still.

Far below, the valley slept beneath a quilt of mist, wrapped in warmth and ritual. Fires burned low and clocks ticked toward comfort. The faint scent of pine and chimney smoke drifted through the hollows.

But high above, the ridges leaned into the wind. The air was sharp enough to bite. Frost slicked every stone, and the streams whispered quietly beneath their thin skin of ice.

Someone was coming.

A man with too much on his shoulders and too little in his pack.

A man chasing the kind of silence that might finally stop the noise inside him.

He did not yet know what he would find – only that something in him had answered the mountain's call, the same call it had been sending out for years without words.

The wind rose, carrying with it the faintest tremor – as though the mountain itself had drawn breath.

The first crunch of boots on frost echoed faintly through the ravines, and the silence, for the briefest moment, seemed to listen back.

And so, beneath a sky that held both storm and promise, he began to climb.

The mountain was waiting.

And had been, all along.

CHAPTER ONE
THE EMPTY SEAT AT THE TABLE

Tom Briggs had never hated tinsel until this year. He used to like the way it caught the light. Those little flashes of silver had made even tired shop windows look hopeful. But this year, it just felt sharp. Artificial. It glinted at him from every corner – shopfronts, buses, café windows – like a joke he wasn't in on. Even the lampposts seemed smug, wrapped in red and gold like they were off to a Christmas that actually meant something.

The world felt overdecorated. Overcompensating. He couldn't remember the last time he'd felt that December flutter – the easy warmth that used to come with the smell of mince pies or the first few bars of a Christmas song in a café. Now, everything felt choreographed. Like the world was performing joy for an audience that had stopped believing in it. He wondered when, exactly, he'd stepped offstage. He'd been moving through life like a ghost at his own wake – present, but never quite in focus.

Some days he wasn't sure if he missed her or the version of himself that existed when she was still around. He'd lost count of the number of times he almost texted her but didn't. And was beginning to feel like a place-holder in his own story, waiting for the plot to pick up again.

He passed a florist with a chalkboard sign that read, *Christmas Eve Bouquets*. Chalk dust smudged the tail of the *s* like a comet.

A child in a reindeer jumper pressed their nose to the glass. Inside, a woman with frost-pink cheeks picked out holly sprigs and eucalyptus.

He turned the corner and walked past the pub – *The Red Lion*. A large sign out front promised mulled wine, a roaring fire, and *Christmas spirit on tap*. There was a wreath on the door, lopsided and wilting, with a few berries missing.

Through the windows, the place was half full, with bodies wrapped in woolly Christmas jumpers and noise. The kind of noise that you only notice when you're not part of it – laughter, clinks of glasses, and the soft cracks of party poppers.

Someone had drawn a crude smiley face into the condensation, and he found himself staring at it longer than he meant to. The sound of a cheer burst suddenly through the door as someone came out for a cigarette, laughter tumbling into the street. Then the door swung shut, and the quiet rushed back in, finding him again.

A few years ago, they'd gone there on Christmas Eve. Mistletoe hung over the jukebox, and someone kept putting 'Fairytale of New York' on repeat. Clare had worn a ridiculous jumper with flashing lights in the antlers and tried to convince him to sing karaoke. He'd refused, of course, but she'd gone up anyway, laughing through the verses of 'Last Christmas'. He'd filmed it. She'd made him delete it the next day, but he hadn't. He wasn't sure he ever could.

She'd bought them Baileys at the bar and called it *Christmas milk*, winking as she took a sip like she was getting away with something.

That was Clare – childlike and cheeky and warm in all the places he wasn't.

He could still hear her laugh when he let her steal his Yorkshire pudding that night, declaring it a festive crime not to serve them. That memory hovered behind the glass. Behind the warmth and the noise and the bodies gathered too close on mismatched chairs. A ghost of what was. Of who he used to be, when her hand was still in his, and the world still felt like something he wanted to be part of.

Outside, near the corner shop, a couple were locked in a low, heated argument over a last-minute present. She held up a novelty shaving kit as he waved a discounted bottle of aftershave like it was evidence in a trial. Their voices rose and fell in bursts that carried across the road. Tom slowed without meaning to, caught in the familiar rhythm of bickering that came from knowing someone too well. He'd forgotten how arguments could be a form of intimacy – two people still bothering to care enough to disagree. These days, even his thoughts didn't argue back. They just looped, quiet and unfinished.

Once, he and Clare had done the same – panicking on Christmas Eve and laughing at the terrible choices left on the shelves. The memory came uninvited, sharp as frost. He quickened his pace.

On the next corner, slumped against the shutter of a closed betting shop, sat a man in a paper Santa hat. The red dye had bled where the rain had caught it, leaving faint stains across his forehead. The man looked up as

Tom passed. His eyes were dull but searching, as if checking whether the world still saw him. Tom knew that look too well.

A takeaway cup rattled weakly by his side. Tom's hand twitched toward his pocket, but he let it fall again. He couldn't even summon kindness for himself; how could he offer it to someone else? The guilt rose, but he walked on anyway. The sound of the rattling cup followed him until the traffic drowned it out.

A bus roared past, brakes squealing as it slowed for the stop. Its windows were steamed. Soft-edged silhouettes shifted and laughed from behind the glass. For a second, one of them looked like Clare. Tom blinked hard, but the bus had already moved on, carrying the warmth and the noise away with it. The red taillights smeared across wet tarmac like two bright commas in a sentence he couldn't finish.

By the time he reached the entrance to his building, his hands were completely frostbitten. The postbox was empty. Again. No cards. No second chances.

As he fumbled with his keys, a voice burst beside

him.

'Evening, Tom!'

He flinched, nearly dropping the keys, and turned to find Sadie from the third floor suddenly at his elbow, cheeks glowing from the cold. She was laden with paper bags that clinked faintly with bottles, tins of biscuits wedged under one arm, and a stray roll of wrapping paper jutting out at an awkward angle.

'Oh! Sorry, love,' she chirped, laughing as she shifted the bags higher. 'Just back from a last-minute dash. You know how it is.'

She gave him a wide smile – the kind people saved for neighbours they barely knew but wanted to keep on side. Tom managed a weak nod, but before he could find any words, she was already clattering up the stairs, still talking to herself about matcha tea, Christmas pudding, and batteries.

The hallway smelt faintly of curry and pine air freshener. From behind one door came the sound of wrapping paper tearing. From another, the tinny echo of a sitcom laugh track. Every door he passed felt like another small, lit world he wasn't part of.

He didn't bother pressing the lift. He took the stairs, two at a time, like the act of getting home faster might change how it felt when he got there.

The stairwell light flickered and made everything look a fraction out of time.

His flat was quiet. Too quiet.

It was the kind of silence that didn't just sit – it crouched, heavy and waiting, like something was about to break.

He dropped his keys into the bowl by the door. They clattered, far too loud for the room. He didn't bother taking off his coat.

The Christmas tree, still boxed and sealed with last year's duct tape, sat untouched in the corner of the living room, where it had been dumped the first weekend of December. He'd moved around it ever since as if it were a piece of furniture instead of a symbol of everything he couldn't bring himself to do.

From somewhere above, muffled through the ceiling, came a burst of laughter and the faint thump of music. Sadie's flat. She was probably unpacking those bags now, tins rattling as she stacked them in cupboards, and her radio blaring out some cheery countdown to Christmas.

The sounds grew into a kind of accidental soundtrack – chairs scraping, feet shuffling, and the thud of something heavy being dragged across the floor.

Laughter rang out again, tangled with the unmistakable opening notes of Mariah Carey. The sounds of domestic chaos and celebration leaked down into his quiet flat as if to taunt him with what he lacked.

He hadn't sent a single card this year. Hadn't bought a gift. Hadn't even pretended to care.

The only 'decoration' was a string of dusty fairy lights that still clung limply to the kitchen window, left by the previous tenant. They hadn't worked since he moved in, but he'd never taken them down. Maybe a part of him liked the futility of them. Like him, they had once been meant for something better.

He set his shopping bags on the counter. Their thin plastic handles were stretched and sharp-edged and had cut into his fingers.

A carton of oat milk, a box of cereal, and a multipack of crisps he didn't really like. He unpacked slowly, without ceremony, letting the fridge door hang open too long. The cold light made the shelves look even barer.

At the bottom of the second bag was the thing he hadn't meant to buy.

He'd picked it up from the reduced section at the

supermarket on his way home. One of those *festive-for-one* meals, marked down with a yellow sticker. He hadn't intended to buy anything Christmassy. But he felt sorry for the way the ready meals were displayed – like tired performers at the end of a pantomime season. Or, perhaps, like they were pretending to be part of a celebration they'd been left out of. Sad and a little ashamed to still be there, lined up under the harsh fluorescent lights above them as if hoping someone might take pity. He lingered longer than he meant to, staring down at them like they might meet his gaze.

They looked the way he felt – past their prime and just about holding it together.

So, he took one. Not because he wanted one, but because, somehow, it felt like the right thing to do. They were cheaper than a takeaway, too, and at least vaguely seasonal. He couldn't stomach the thought of ordering from the curry place again, especially not after last Christmas Eve, when she'd texted halfway through his paneer jalfrezi to say she was spending Christmas Day with someone else.

Without much thought, he tore off the cardboard sleeve, peeled back the film with a sigh, and slid the plastic tray into the microwave. It hummed as the plastic film ballooned like a blister. He stood with his arms folded, staring at it like it might confess something.

In the other corner of his small apartment, the radiator clicked and gurgled to itself, trying and failing to be useful.

A bottle of whisky stood untouched by the kitchen sink. Supermarket own-brand. Cheap and bitter. He'd picked it up two days ago, thinking he might drink it in front of the telly on Christmas Day, maybe stick on *It's a Wonderful Life* and sneer through the whole thing. But he hadn't even cracked the seal; the idea of getting drunk alone on Christmas had lost its romance this year. Now it just felt like maintenance. Like changing a lightbulb in a room nobody used anymore.

On the nearby table, a single paper crown lay folded and faded. Last year's. From a cracker he'd pulled by himself after a two-hour walk that led nowhere. He'd kept it, but he wasn't sure why. Defiance, maybe. Or forgetfulness. These days, the difference was hard to tell.

He pulled out a chair and sat heavily, letting the quiet press in around him. He could almost hear Clare's voice cutting across it. Telling him off for forgetting the napkins. Mocking the way he always overcooked sprouts. Smirking as she said, 'Tell me again how Yorkshire puddings aren't for Christmas dinner. I dare you!'

But it was only a memory. Or imagination. Either

way, it wasn't enough.

His phone buzzed.

He didn't need to look. He knew who it would be.

When he did, there it was – *Mum* lighting up the screen, as if her name alone might fix things.

You can still come tomorrow, darling. Your stocking's waiting. x

He didn't answer. Just stared until the screen dimmed again, casting him back into shadow.

There would be a seat at their table. There always was. And he could picture it all so clearly – his mum making bread sauce from scratch, like she did every year, his dad in the kitchen, apron on, peeling potatoes with military precision, and Bing Crosby on the radio. His dad would overcook the pigs in blankets because he forgot they were in the oven again, and his mum would bring up the time he was five and thought Santa had left him a cassette tape because he'd been a good boy. Anything not to mention Clare's name. Anything but the truth. It had always been chaos. But it had been *his* chaos. And now he didn't know if he belonged in it anymore.

He stood and walked to the microwave. He opened the door and took the dinner out early. He didn't even glance at the food. Just threw the whole thing into the bin. The smell of plastic and processed gravy clung to the air as he did.

He opened the fridge, half out of habit.

A piece of cheese starting to grow mould. A crumpled packet of ham. A jar of mustard. A chutney his mum had given him in September, unopened, like so many things between them.

And there, wedged in sideways, almost comically out of place, was a spring onion.

Bent and wilted slightly at the neck, like it had been trying to stand tall for too long.

He stared at it for longer than he meant to.

It looked ridiculous. Lonely. A leftover from a life that had involved stir-fries and shopping lists. The kind of vegetable that expected to be chopped and tossed into something fragrant, not forgotten on the top shelf behind a jar of sadness.

Clare used to throw them into everything – stir-fries, omelettes, and even sandwiches. She'd laugh at the way he always bought too many. There were always bunches wilting in the fridge by the week's end.

'You think you're feeding a family of six, Tom?' she'd tease, chopping them down to neat rings with quick, confident hands.

He could almost hear the slice of the knife on the board and the sizzle as she tossed them into a pan.

And then there were the onions. He remembered her hair tied back in a messy knot, strands falling across her forehead. She used to wear those ridiculous plastic goggles – the ones she swore stopped her crying when she chopped. He'd teased her every time, but she'd grin through the lenses and keep going, knife tapping a steady rhythm against the board. The memory stung sharper than any onion ever had.

Now there was just this one spring onion, bent and forgotten, pretending to belong.

He shut the door gently.

He didn't eat. He didn't drink. He stood in the centre of the room, then slowly crossed to the living area and pulled open the drawer beneath the bookcase. Inside, a mess of old chargers, rubber bands, takeaway menus, and a faded photo of him and Clare standing on a rock in the Lake District, soaked to the skin and smiling. She had her arm around his neck, and he was holding up a thermos like a trophy. The clouds were low behind them. Misty. Romantic in that damp, English way.

He looked at the photo for a long time. Long enough that his fingers went cold.

Then he put it back.

He opened another drawer. Pulled out a tattered Ordnance Survey map. Its edges were torn and stained with old mud and time. He unfolded it carefully and reverently, like a priest handling relics.

His fingers found the spot instantly. They always did.

Scafell Pike.

It wasn't a name that invited warmth; he had once climbed it with Clare. They'd taken the wrong path and ended up waist-deep in water, laughing like idiots. She'd worn the worst boots imaginable. He'd brought the wrong gloves. They'd shared a thermos and a terrible flapjack and kissed at the summit as the clouds parted like theatre curtains.

She'd cried and called it perfect.

He had kissed the tears from her cheek.

And he'd believed it would always feel that way.

That felt like someone else's memory now. A postcard he'd picked up by mistake.

He traced the trail on the map with one finger. Up from Wasdale. A slow, hard climb.

This time, there would be no tears. No thermos of hot chocolate. No Clare.

This time, he would climb alone.

Not for the view.

Not even for the challenge.

But for the silence. The stillness. The hope that if

he got high enough, the ache in his chest might quieten down.

Or freeze over entirely.

He stared at the map until his eyes blurred, then refolded it carefully, smoothing each crease.

He didn't tell anyone where he was going. He didn't draft a text. He didn't leave a note. He just packed a bag and went to bed, fully dressed, boots by the door, and ready for an early start.

And when he woke in the middle of the night – before the birds, before the sun, before any sensible reason not to – he picked up the bag and headed to the front door.

But something pulled him back.

The fridge.

The spring onion.

He stood in front of it for a second time, not opening the door, just thinking.

Then, he turned the handle and reached in.

It came away cold in his hand, damp from condensation.

He held it for a moment, studying its limp neck and its faint scent. It smelt of very little. Maybe that was the point.

It wasn't practical. It wasn't even logical. But neither was grief. Some things you kept because you weren't ready to let go.

He wrapped it loosely in a sandwich bag and took it with him.

Not for eating.

Just ... because.

Something green in a grey world.

Something alive.

CHAPTER TWO
THE ROAD NORTH

The roads were quiet on Christmas morning. No headlights in the mirrors. No sounds other than the engine and the dull rhythm of tyres on tarmac. His 2008 Peugeot – scratched, dented, smelling faintly of old pine air freshener, and coughing like a lifelong smoker – rattled along the M6. He drove with both hands on the wheel, his shoulders hunched, and his eyes fixed on the road ahead with hollow concentration.

The heating didn't work properly – the fan made a high-pitched whine, and every few minutes the windscreen fogged up. He'd wipe it with the sleeve of his coat, which only made it worse, smearing condensation in arcs across his view.

Out of habit more than hope, he flicked the radio on. A cheery DJ burst through the static, counting down Christmas hits before a hymn swelled in the background, all bells and choirs. The noise scraped at him, and he snapped the radio off again. The silence that followed was worse, but at least it was honest.

The road ahead shimmered faintly under the streetlights, a tunnel of grey and nothing else. He felt like the last person left awake in England. Everyone else was dreaming. Everyone else was safe.

A few miles on, the motorway diverted through a village that lay utterly still. Not a light in the houses and not a sound behind the curtained windows. In the square, beneath the harsh glare of a single streetlamp, stood a plastic nativity. Mary and Joseph stared blankly through scratched faces, their colours bleached by too many winters. A sheep had toppled sideways in the straw, legs jutting like it had been struck down mid-step. The only movement came from a flickering bulb inside the baby Jesus, flaring, dying, and flaring again, like a heartbeat on its last warning.

He wondered if anyone would notice when the light finally went out for good, or if it would just flicker quietly into darkness like everything else.

Someone had tried. Someone had bent over this display in the wet December air, cable-tying plastic saints together, tucking hay where it would never stay dry.

Tom slowed as he passed, the figures glowing faintly through the mist. For a second, he thought of pulling over just to stand there. Just to feel close to something that claimed to mean hope. But the feeling passed. Hope belonged to other people.

He pressed the accelerator, and the fragile glow of the manger sank into the fog behind him.

He'd never been religious, not really, but there was something about that dim glow that lodged under his skin. Maybe it wasn't faith he missed, but the comfort of believing someone, somewhere, was keeping watch. The kind of belief that made you feel less alone in the dark.

He stopped at a 24-hour service station somewhere near Rugby, its forecourt lit like an operating theatre. Inside, the smell of burnt coffee and diesel hung in the air. A couple in Santa hats were laughing by the pastry cabinet, their laughter too loud for the hour. He bought a coffee from the machine, the cup trembling slightly as it filled, and stood by the window watching the road. He didn't drink it. The heat only made the ache in his chest more obvious. When he left, his reflection followed him in the glass until the automatic doors closed.

There was something about driving alone in the dark that made it harder to lie to himself. To pretend he was okay. No cheerful small talk to distract himself. No half-smiles or polite eyebrow raises. Just a long stretch of road and the truth pressing in from all sides.

He'd spent months pretending he was fine, telling his parents, colleagues, and even himself that he was 'doing all right, considering.' Making the odd joke. Laughing at the right moments. It was easier than admitting he felt like he was dying inside.

That was the thing about depression – it didn't always look like silence or sadness. Sometimes it appeared as too many jokes and oversharing – revealing more than intended in the break room just to feel a flicker of something meaningful.

It wasn't really about telling people too much – it was more about slipping truths into conversations and testing the waters for some recognition. To be seen. For something that felt like it could be a genuine connection. But that connection never came. And, alone in the car, only silence listened. And it didn't speak back.

His mind went down a rabbit hole, spiralling through old echoes and grasping at things that were already gone.

Clare.

She surfaced like she always did – without warning and impossible to push back down. Her laugh and her handwriting on the last Post-it note still stuck to the fridge. The way she used to tuck her feet under his legs on the sofa, like it was the most natural thing in the world to make a home inside someone else's warmth.

She used to sit where the passenger seat was now empty, one hand always finding his or resting lightly on his lap. The quiet between them had never felt lonely back then – it was just easy, like breathing.

On long drives, she'd insist on a podcast about something topical, or Radio 2 if she couldn't decide. Sometimes, when the road was smooth and the world felt far away, she'd rest her head on his shoulder and close her eyes. Nobody had ever done that before – trusted him like that or made stillness feel like enough. She'd hum sometimes, softly and off-key, just enough for him to feel it through his shoulder. He'd find himself matching his breathing to hers without even meaning to. It was the kind of closeness you never notice until it's gone. Now, the same dashboard light that once touched her face only caught the emptiness beside him.

He reached over sometimes, without thinking, fingertips brushing the worn leather of the seat as if it might still be warm. Habit more than hope. The ghost of muscle memory.

He remembered another drive, years ago, to the coast. Clare had fallen asleep halfway there, her hand still resting in his. The sea was grey when they arrived, the wind cruel, but she'd called it perfect anyway. He'd driven slower on the way back, hoping to keep her asleep a little longer, her breath rising and falling against the hum of the engine.

He remembered her one Christmas, dragging him through a market in town with tinsel in her hair and an armful of shopping bags. She'd stop at every stall, making him try free samples of mince pies and declaring each one the best yet. He'd grumble and insist they all tasted the same, but she'd just laugh and press another one into his hand until his coat pockets were full of crumbs. Her delight was impossible to resist, even when he tried.

He thought about that New Year's Eve, a few years

back, when they'd decided not to go out.

'Let's do canapés,' she'd said, 'like we're at a party, but just for us.'

He'd spent over an hour making tiny penguins out of olives, mozzarella balls, and slivers of carrot. She'd laughed so hard when she saw them, she nearly dropped the prosecco.

'You're ridiculous,' she'd said, kissing him on the cheek. 'These are going on Instagram.'

'Absolutely not,' he'd replied. 'They're emotionally fragile.'

After midnight, they'd slow-danced in the kitchen in their socks, and she'd whispered, 'You're my penguin.'

He really loved her. Not the romcom kind with airport chases and big speeches, but in the quiet, steady way that makes life feel less like surviving and more like belonging.

She saw the best in everyone and in everything, and she was always smiling.

She'd find joy in even the smallest things, like the first daffodil in the spring or a well-organised sock drawer.

He'd once joked that she couldn't walk into a room without rearranging it. She'd laughed and said she was *Clare-ifying* it. Within weeks, his flat had plants, throw cushions, and light that seemed to find corners it had ignored for years.

She used to leave Post-it notes around the flat, too. Sometimes on the fridge, sometimes tucked inside his coat pocket, and sometimes slipped into his shoes.

You're stronger than you think.

I love your weird brain.

He used to tease her for it, but he'd kept every single one.

She had a way of looking after him without making it feel like pity. She'd rein him in gently when his mind wobbled, reminding him who he was when he forgot. When the world felt too sharp, she softened the edges.

She also loved to clean – *really* clean – and organise everything in sight. Once, he came home to find all his shirts arranged by colour and sleeve length. He'd smiled at the sticky note she'd left on the wardrobe door.

You're welcome. Your chaos stresses me out.

She said tidying helped her feel calm and that she liked the idea of creating order where there was none. He said she'd missed her calling as a librarian-slash-miracle worker.

He left her notes too, but his were more functional, like reminders about milk or dentist appointments. She kept those as well. Stuffed in a drawer next to birthday cards and the warranty for the toaster because that was her – someone who saved even the ordinary things, just in case they turned out to be important.

There hadn't been an explosion.

No final fight. No dramatic ending.

Just a slow, quiet drift into missed calls, messages left on read, and nights she'd come home later than before. Eventually, the *I love you*s stopped being returned. And Tom felt like he lived with a stranger and was speaking into an empty void.

And then, one morning, the truth.

She'd met someone else.

Or maybe she'd already known him.

Tom still wasn't sure what hurt more – what she did, or how carefully she tried not to hurt him while doing it.

She'd cried when she told him. Not the kind of tears that begged forgiveness, but the quiet, exhausted kind that came from having held it all in for too long. Like the truth had finally worn her down and had leaked out.

It had been a Tuesday. He remembered because of the toast. He'd burnt it. Not badly. Just enough to set off the smoke alarm.

She'd come downstairs in a dressing gown, her hair twisted up with a pencil – he always loved when she did that – and then it happened.

Out of nowhere.

No build-up.

Just: 'I need to tell you something.'

At first, he thought someone had died.

He remembered the way her fingers played with the drawstring of her robe. The way she looked everywhere but at him.

And then she said the name. A name he didn't recognise. A colleague. A conference. A hotel with paper-thin walls.

He hadn't said anything at first. He'd just stared at her like she'd spoken in another language. As if he'd misheard.

And then, finally: 'Why?'

She'd shrugged. Actually shrugged. And then the

shrug turned into something else – an ache at the corners of her mouth. A kind of apology that never reached her eyes.

'I felt invisible,' she whispered. 'For a long time.'

That part hurt more than the betrayal itself. Because it was true.

He'd been distracted for months. Work. Life. That stupid spreadsheet he kept saying he had to finish. The one he could no longer even remember the purpose of. He hadn't seen her properly. Not really. And when he did, it was too late.

And now, here he was, halfway up the M6 with a boot full of regrets and a spring onion in his glovebox, heading for the one place stupid enough to match his mood.

He joined the A595, passing the sign for Kendal. He kept going, hands stiff on the wheel and the cabin cold despite the struggling heater.

His phone buzzed in the passenger seat, the screen lighting up with the word *Mum*.

He hesitated. Then swiped to answer.

'Tom?' Her voice was quiet but awake. Alert.

'Hi, Mum.'

'I didn't wake you, did I?'

'No. I've been driving.'

A pause.

'I thought so,' she said softly. 'I woke up and just ... had a feeling. That you'd gone somewhere. Are you all right?'

'I'm fine,' he said. Too quickly. 'Just needed some air. A bit of space.'

'On Christmas morning?'

He didn't answer.

'You didn't have to be alone, love.'

'I know.' Another pause. 'I just ... didn't know where else to go.'

She exhaled gently, and he could picture her sitting at the kitchen table in her dressing gown, tea gone cold in her hands.

'At least tell me you're somewhere safe.'

'I'm nearly there. I'll be careful.'

'Please let me know when you're there. Just a quick message.'

'I will.'

'Tom...'

'Yeah?'

'Love you.'

He smiled despite himself. 'Love you, too.'

He ended the call before she could ask anything else.

The signal dropped moments later as the valley narrowed around him.

The sun hadn't risen yet, but the sky was turning purple. He opened the glovebox and glanced at the spring onion, still wrapped in the sandwich bag that had once held better things. Back when it carried slices of manchego and sourdough, packed by Clare for weekend hikes. Or leftover brownies she'd made after one of his bad days, still warm in the middle and tasting like comfort.

A ridiculous thing to bring. But then again, grief made you do strange things. It was shrivelled now. He should have thrown it out. But some part of him thought he might still need it. Like a spare key to a door that no longer existed. Maybe it reminded him of something. Of cooking with Clare. Of the life he'd once had; they used to cook together, back in the early days. She'd chop onions. He'd read the recipe aloud, even though they both knew it by heart.

They'd danced once to the timer beeping, her barefoot in the kitchen and with flour on her nose.

The road narrowed as he turned off the A595. The lake to his left glimmered weakly in the half-light, like a closed eye refusing to wake. Wasdale came into view, or rather it didn't – it was mostly mist and shape, the mountains hidden behind a curtain of fog.

Tom almost overshot the turn to Scafell Pike, his attention drifting for just a moment as the road ahead blurred into a maze of twists and turns. The narrow, uneven path was easy to miss, and his tyres skidded slightly as he pulled the wheel sharply, catching the road just in time.

The drive became slow, the car bouncing over potholes and uneven patches; the path seemed more suggestion than surface. Alongside, the landscape unfurled in sweeping vistas, but there was something unsettling about it today. The usually majestic mountains were shrouded, their outlines soft and elusive, as though they might dissolve into the fog at any moment.

The rugged terrain of the valley floor was dotted with scattered grazing sheep, their pale bodies blending into the landscape like ghostly apparitions, the only movement the faint sway of grass in the wind.

The way ahead seemed distant, almost unreachable, and yet the car park at the base of Scafell Pike was close now – it was just beyond the last stretch of rough, narrow road.

His journey wasn't just from Wasdale to Scafell Pike. It was a crossing from the flat, ordinary world to something wild, untamed, and untouched.

He arrived at the car park – a small area of gravel with just a few spaces lined up along its edge, but with the weight of hundreds of climbers' stories embedded into it. It was deserted. He rolled to a stop beneath a tree, switched off the engine, and listened.

Silence.

Not city silence – the kind that's never quite still. But rural silence. Total. Untouched. The kind that made you aware of your own breath.

He didn't move for a while. Just sat. Fingers still on the wheel. Like if he let go, something in him would come undone.

He hadn't come to feel better. He'd come to feel

something. Or maybe nothing. Either would be a relief.

No one else was here. Not even a stray hiker. Not even a dog walker or an early jogger pretending to be festive with a Santa hat.

The ground was wet from an early rain, puddles reflecting ghostly fragments of the mist. Even the trees, normally alive with the rustling of leaves, stood still, their branches reaching like hands that couldn't touch.

The silence felt too complete, as if the world was holding its breath, waiting for something to happen. Or maybe waiting for nothing at all.

He stepped out of the car and into the cold. It slapped his cheeks and crawled up his sleeves. There was no sound except for the faint, distant call of a bird, or perhaps just the wind playing tricks. He hesitated, unsure whether the fog was hiding what he sought or simply taking it away.

He spotted a lone outdoor tap beside a weathered outbuilding near the edge of the car park – a ranger's office, probably, long since locked up for Christmas. A hand-painted sign above the door read *Wasdale Mountain Rescue*. He walked over stiffly, unscrewing his empty water bottle with fingers that didn't want to move. When he turned the tap, it sputtered and groaned before releasing a thin stream of water, icy enough to sting.

He fumbled the bottle as he tried to fill it, his hands shaking from the cold, the plastic slipping from his grip and clattering to the gravel. He swore under his breath, picked it up, and tried again.

It took longer than it should have. Everything took longer when you were this cold and unprepared. No gloves. No map. No plan. Just layers that didn't match, and boots that hadn't seen mud in years. The kind of hike most people trained for, he was doing because he didn't know what else to do.

He zipped his coat up to his chin and tightened the straps of his backpack. He headed for the trailhead sign, worn and barely legible.

Then, he began his ascent.

And with every step, he left something behind:

The empty bed.

The unopened bottle of whisky.

The stocking at his parents' house.

The version of himself that had believed you could love someone into staying.

He didn't want peace. Not really.

He wanted stillness.

He wanted the cold to numb him clean.

The mountain welcomed no one. And that was precisely what he needed.

This was it.

No witnesses. No invitations. No second thoughts.

Just a man and a mountain.

CHAPTER THREE
THE LOST PATH

The first part of the climb was manageable.

Not easy – his calves protested almost immediately – but manageable. The path had been trodden by enough boots to leave a faint scar through the landscape, just visible enough to follow.

The silence out here was deeper than he'd expected and strangely comforting. Just the sound of his boots as he moved steadily, one step at a time. Behind him, the car park had already vanished into the mist.

He hadn't eaten breakfast. A mistake, maybe; he was feeling lightheaded. Though it could've been the altitude. Or the climb. Or just the heaviness of everything he wasn't ready to name.

He remembered another climb, years ago – a smaller, warmer climb somewhere in the Peak District. They'd set off from Hathersage just after dawn. The air was still damp with mist and the scent of wet grass. The path wound upward through bracken and ferns – the kind that brushed against your legs and left a trace of dew behind.

He'd brought along a brand-new 360-degree camera. It was one of those gadgets he'd convinced himself he *needed*. Clare had rolled her eyes the moment he unpacked it from its protective case. They'd argued halfway up about it. Or, rather, she'd laughed at his insistence on setting it up every few metres.

'We could just enjoy the view,' Clare had said, grinning as she waited for him to finish fiddling with the tripod.

'We *are* enjoying it,' he'd protested. 'I'm capturing memories.'

'You're missing them,' she'd replied, stepping into the frame just as the shutter clicked.

She hardly ever looked at the camera when her picture was taken. It was one of those small, sometimes infuriating quirks that made her *her* – head turned, hair in her face, always laughing at something outside the frame. Somehow, those were the photos he loved most.

By the time they reached the ridge, the argument had dissolved. The view spread in every direction. It was the kind of panorama that made you forget where you'd started.

A pair of walkers passed them, nodding their hellos, and Clare waved like they were old friends.

She handed him a flask of coffee that had leaked through her bag, soaking her jumper, and they both laughed. The steam from the flask rose between them, curling into the cool air.

'We're lost,' she'd said, brushing at the stain. 'But at least the view's decent.'

He'd loved that about her – the way she could turn being lost into a kind of home. How her warmth could make even the wildest places feel like they belonged to them.

After about forty minutes, he paused, leaning against a rock to catch his breath. The slope had steepened, and snow was beginning to fall. The kind that didn't seem serious until it started to settle.

The air grew sharper, biting at the inside of his nose until each breath felt like inhaling glass.

His watch fogged with condensation, time slowing to a crawl that didn't match his pulse. He couldn't tell if it was ten in the morning or already evening. The mountain distorted everything – distance, sound, and the sense of how long he'd been alone.

He unscrewed his water bottle with stiff fingers and took a sip. Metallic, but clean.

He hadn't packed food. No snacks. No map. No gloves. No plan. Just the foolish hope that walking uphill might drown out the noise in his head.

He was underprepared. He knew that. And he knew that Scafell Pike was the hardest of the Three Peaks to navigate, especially in winter. No well-defined path. No reliable signage. Even seasoned climbers had been caught out here. And Tom wasn't a seasoned climber – he was a man with sore feet, in boots two sizes too big, and with no idea what he was really doing.

He looked at the rock he was still leaning against. A single bead of water caught his eye, clinging to the uneven surface beside him. It trembled for a moment before beginning to slide down the stone.

It was just like the drop that had trickled down the neck of a Heineken bottle she'd been holding the first time he saw her at his brother's birthday barbecue.

Clare had been laughing at her own joke about potatoes, sitting on a garden wall with one leg tucked under the other. He'd offered her the last sausage without speaking, then panicked about how awkward that was.

'Are you always this generous with meat products?' she'd teased.

'Only with the right people,' he'd replied, instantly mortified.

She'd smiled, eyes crinkling. 'Well. Lucky me.'

Tom pushed away from the rock and continued on, rounding a bend where two sheep stood motionless on the trail. One lifted its head slowly, blinked, then returned to chewing a patch of frost-hardened grass.

'Morning,' he muttered, voice hoarse. 'Guess it's just us out here.'

The sheep blinked again, unimpressed.

They were the only living things he'd seen all morning. It struck him as oddly reassuring, and then oddly sad that the only company he had was two sheep too indifferent to care whether he lived or died.

'What am I doing?' he whispered.

The sheep didn't answer.

They reminded him, absurdly, of that windswept beach in Cornwall. Their first holiday. She'd insisted on going out despite the storm. They'd trudged through the sand in ponchos, her hair plastered to her cheeks, laughing at the sheep on the hillside watching them.

'You think they're wondering if we're stupid or brave?' she'd asked, tugging her hood tight against the wind.

'Both,' he'd said. 'Definitely both.'

That night, back in their Airbnb, the power had gone out. They'd lit candles and played chess on a wobbly wooden table.

'I could do this forever,' he'd said.

She'd kissed his forehead. 'Then let's try.'

A little further up Scafell Pike, the path met a stream. It caught him off guard; he didn't remember this from last time. The flow of water was fast and rushed over jagged rocks. There were stepping stones, but not many, and most were slick with ice. He stood at the edge for a long time, weighing up his options. A misstep wouldn't kill him, but it would soak him. Chill him. Knock the fight out of him before he'd really begun.

He picked a route. The first two steps were fine. The third one wasn't. He slipped. For a split second he was weightless – arms flailing like a cartoon – and then his right foot plunged into the stream. He gasped as ice-cold water filled his boot, soaking his sock. He staggered across the final stones, the soaked foot squelching with every step.

Once on the other side, he stopped and collected his thoughts. The mountain didn't care why he was here. It would take from him just the same.

He stood there for a moment, chest heaving, and was reminded of their first week living together. The pipe had burst under the kitchen sink without warning. One second he was reaching for a tea towel; the next he was drenched and swearing, water pooling around his feet.

She'd burst into the room barefoot, slid across the lino like it was a skating rink, and laughed the whole way through it.

'The plumbing's shocking,' she'd said cheerfully, grabbing a saucepan to catch the spray.

She wasn't wrong. The water pressure was hopeless, the shower took twenty minutes to warm up, and the radiators clicked like they were plotting something.

But she had made the flat a home.

She'd painted the walls a different colour in every room and had brought home a 'happy' plant pot with a smiley face on it, setting it on the windowsill in the kitchen. Inside it was a fern she'd affectionately named Janice.

'She's a happy pot,' Clare said. 'You can't be miserable with Janice in the room.'

And, somehow, he hadn't been.

He remembered their first Christmas there together. Snow had fallen that week, the kind that dusted rooftops and turned the roads to slush before midday. Clare had insisted it was 'proper Christmas snow,' even when it had all melted before lunchtime.

That was the year she'd bought the soup maker. A colleague at work had sworn by it, calling it 'life changing.' From the moment it arrived, Clare was evangelical about it. Every conversation somehow led back to soup. She'd stand in the kitchen with her hair pulled into a lopsided bun, tipping in whatever she could find in the fridge, declaring herself a 'culinary alchemist.' Half the time it worked. The other half, they pretended it did.

'Carrot and pear,' she'd announced one night, triumphantly pouring steaming orange liquid into mismatched mugs. 'Trust me – I'm basically a soup genius.'

He had, and it had tasted like confusion. She'd laughed so hard she nearly spilt it.

Soon, everyone was getting soup. Friends, neighbours, even the postman once. She'd fill recycled jars with whatever concoction she'd made that day, stick a Post-it note on the lid with a doodled smiley face, and send Tom out with deliveries.

'Everyone needs a little warmth,' she'd say, and he'd believe her.

When the pipes froze that winter, they'd worn woolly hats indoors and eaten soup for breakfast – an experiment that had turned out surprisingly decent. She'd said it was romantic. He'd said it was ridiculous. She'd kissed him anyway, her nose cold, her lips warm.

The sun broke through just for a moment, scattering light across the valley. A brief, bright window. He continued to climb up the mountain as the snow returned with a sudden thickening.

Within minutes, visibility dropped. The horizon

vanished. The trail, already vague, became guesswork. The air turned white. The ground turned white. His footprints disappeared behind him almost instantly.

But he kept going.

The wind tore sideways across the path. His wet sock began to freeze around his foot, the chill numbing his toes. His fingers throbbed in time with his pulse.

Every few steps, he had to stop. Turn in a slow circle. Try to make sense of the shadows. Squint into the blur of white and try to guess which direction felt *less wrong* than the others.

He stopped. There were footprints ahead of him in the snow, fading where the wind had tried to erase them. For a moment, his breath caught; someone else was up there with him. Relief rose, unsteady but real, through the exhaustion. He wasn't alone.

He took a few steps closer, squinting through the blur of falling snow. The prints trailed off around a bend, half-filled already, soft-edged and fading fast. He followed them, calling out once, his voice thin against the wind.

No answer.

When the wind eased for a second, he crouched down and looked more closely. The tread was uneven – the right foot dragging slightly. The same drag as his. He frowned. Then the truth hit him, quiet and heavy.

They were his own footprints.

He'd walked in a circle.

The world tilted slightly. He turned slowly, scanning the white, trying to find where he'd gone wrong – a rock, a marker, any hint of direction – but there was nothing. Just white above, white below, white all around. His breath came out ragged, fogging the air in front of him.

For the first time, real fear settled in. Not the poetic kind he'd come chasing, but the small, practical kind – the kind that reminded you that mountains didn't forgive mistakes.

He laughed once, a sound too sharp to be amusement.

'Brilliant,' he muttered. 'Bloody brilliant.'

The sound was swallowed immediately. Even his own voice refused to stay with him.

Just then, his phone pinged. A single, thin note in the emptiness. He pulled it out with numb fingers, the screen lighting up against the snow. *No signal.* Just an old voicemail icon, waiting, small and insistent in the glow of the screen.

He didn't open it. He didn't need to. He knew exactly who it would be.

The glow of the screen faded, and the mountain closed in again.

He felt like he was shrinking. Not in size, but in certainty. The mountain was swallowing him, bit by bit.

He began talking to Clare aloud.

Not because he thought she was there. But because the silence had turned on him.

'You'd have told me this was a stupid idea,' he muttered.

Then louder: 'You'd have turned back by now.'

A gust of wind answered.

He saw her. Or thought he did. A shape through the snow. A smile. Her red scarf. It vanished the moment he blinked.

He spoke again, quieter this time.

'I miss you.'

Nothing replied.

He kept walking.

The ground beneath him was uneven and crumbling in places. One wrong step could be the edge, and he knew it. Panic began to edge in. Quiet at first. Then louder. He dropped to his hands and knees more than once, crawling blindly over jagged stone, scraping his palms raw.

The cold was no longer something he could ignore. His hands were shaking, his face was numb, and every part of him was afraid.

The wind clawed at him while he fumbled with trembling fingers for his phone again. One bar of signal. He thought about calling mountain rescue for help. Saying he was lost. Freezing. That he hadn't eaten. That he was somewhere near the summit, maybe. That he didn't know which way was down.

But it was Christmas Day.

And the thought of someone leaving their family, their warmth, their paper hats and cranberry sauce for *him* felt unbearable.

He pictured a radio crackling into life in someone's hallway. A volunteer standing up from dinner. A child asking where Mum or Dad was going. So, he slipped the phone back into his pocket clumsily.

Something brushed against his hand.

Paper. Folded.

He pulled it out and stared.

A Post-it note. Creased and slightly faded.

Her handwriting. Slanted. Familiar.

Keep going.

You've got this.

– C x

He blinked at it, barely able to see the words through the fog in his eyes. He hadn't realised it was in his coat. He couldn't even remember when she'd written it.

But he remembered now.

She'd left it on the bathroom mirror before one of his job interviews. He'd peeled it off and pocketed it. Thought he'd lost it. But here it was. Years later. Still folded. Still trying to help.

He stood there momentarily, snow crusting his hair, and he remembered the last note. The one still stuck to the fridge.

I'm sorry.

I need to go.

Take care of yourself.

– C

He refolded the Post-it – the one he'd just found in his coat like it had been waiting – and placed it gently back in the inside pocket.

Then he kept walking.

Not because he wasn't scared. Not because he wasn't lost.

But because she'd told him to.

He blinked through the snow and thought he saw a shape ahead.

He took a step.

Then another.

And then, at last, it came into view.

The trig point.

The summit.

He reached out and touched it.

His legs were shaking. His hands stung.

But he had made it. He was standing on top of England. Above towns. Above rooftops. Above the ache of everything he'd left behind.

And he had brought it all with him.

The grief. The silence. The weight of what he never said.

He expected to feel something more. Triumph. Relief. Vindication.

But what he felt was a strange kind of stillness.

Not peace. Not pride. Just quiet.

He looked out. Just fog. Just white. Just the faintest outline of sky meeting stone.

He had meant to propose.

He'd bought the ring one quiet Tuesday, after watching her sing along to a song while brushing crumbs off the toaster. There was no big epiphany – just the steady, wordless knowing that if he didn't try to make her permanent, he'd regret it.

He kept the box hidden in the sock drawer, beneath old birthday cards.

But the right moment never came. Or maybe it did, and he'd missed it.

She started coming home later. Smiling less. They started to sit on opposite ends of the sofa.

'Are you happy?' he'd asked one night, not sure he wanted to know the answer.

She didn't lie.

'I don't know,' she said. 'I want to be.'

And that, somehow, was worse than if she'd just said 'no.'

It left him hoping. Waiting. Trying to fix something.

He told himself it was a phase. That she was tired. That it would pass.

But deep down, he knew.

So, he never asked. And she never knew.

He stayed at the summit for a long time.

He placed both hands on the trig point, leaned his forehead against the stone, and closed his eyes.

He wanted to believe he'd left something behind on the way up. The doubt. The loneliness. The weight of what-ifs and I-should-haves.

He didn't feel fixed.

He felt eroded. Hollowed out by wind and memory.

The summit hadn't answered anything.

But it had listened.

And maybe, for now, that was enough.

The wind began to push at him gently, as if nudging him back down.

He stepped back. Looked down the slope.

And began the descent.

The snow had covered his tracks. The trail was gone again.

He picked his way down carefully. The slope was steeper and more treacherous now. Rocks were slick with ice. Patches of scree hid beneath snowdrifts.

He moved like someone unsure of their body. His legs shook from the climb. The cold had dulled his senses. His soaked foot was numb and clumsy inside the boot. Still, he pressed on.

A gust of wind slammed into him as he rounded a narrow bend. He staggered and caught himself.

But the next rock was slicker than it looked.

His foot slipped.

His shoulder clipped a jagged stone.

And then he went down. Hard.

His head struck the rock with a sickening, final crack.

Silence.

He lay facedown in the snow, breath stalled, limbs slack.

A thin trickle of blood slid across his temple, vanishing into the whiteness of the snow.

His eyelashes fluttered. Then stilled.

The fog pressed in around him, indifferent.

Somewhere far below, the valley waited. But it didn't know he was missing.

Nobody did.

He had thought, for so long, that disappearing slowly would hurt less than being left. But in the end, it was the same.

The mountain had only listened.

It said nothing.

Just took what it was given.

CHAPTER FOUR
THE MAN IN THE STORM

Tom gasped.

Air rushed in like panic, and his lungs seized it greedily. He coughed before breath found its rhythm, and life returned to his eyes.

Snowflakes clung to his eyelashes. The sky above him was white and featureless. His ears rang and his eyes throbbed. He turned his head, every muscle stiff and unwilling.

A figure sat beside him.

Not leaning over. Not panicked. Just ... there. Calm. Collected. As if he'd been waiting patiently for Tom to rejoin the world.

He wore a navy-blue jacket and a red woollen hat

with a tiny pom-pom.

But what drew Tom's eye, more than anything, was the badge pinned to the man's lapel – a small silver swallow with its wings stretched wide. It shimmered each time the light caught it.

Tom forgot how to breathe.

The swallow.

For a moment, the ringing in his ears stopped, replaced by the memory of the quiet scratch of pen on paper. Clare's handwriting. Her old notebook – the one with the weathered brown cover and the tiny silver bird embossed on the front. She used to say swallows were a sign of hope. That they always found their way home.

'Swallows always come back,' she'd said, nudging him with her shoulder. 'Even after a storm. Even when the world's moved on.'

Tom blinked, disoriented. The snow, the man, and the pain in his head all pressed in again, but something had shifted. The badge had opened a door he'd long kept shut. He wasn't sure if it hurt or healed.

Snow gathered on the man's shoulders like it belonged

there. Like the mountain had made space for him.

He hadn't flinched at Tom's gasp. Hadn't scrambled to help. He had just sat. Finally, he looked over, met Tom's eyes, and asked, lightly,

'You all right?' as if they were sharing a bench in a quiet park instead of lying half-buried on the side of a frozen mountain.

Tom's throat burnt as he tried to answer; he only managed a dry croak. The man unscrewed the top of a flask and handed it over.

'Drink.'

Tom held the flask with both hands, letting the heat bleed into his skin.

The smell was sharp and familiar – bergamot and something floral. Clare used to drink Earl Grey too, though she always left the teabag in too long. He'd teased her for making it taste like perfume. Now, as the warmth spread down his throat, he couldn't help but think of her.

It hit his chest like a flare, igniting something he hadn't realised had gone cold.

'Better?' the man asked.

Tom nodded slightly. 'Who ... are you?'

'Yusuf,' he replied. 'You're Tom.'

It wasn't a question.

Tom blinked. 'Have we met?'

'Not yet.'

A pause.

'You hit your head. You'll be sore as anything, but you're in one piece.'

Tom tried to sit up. He winced. 'How did you find me?'

Yusuf tilted his head. 'I walk. I listen.'

'To what?'

'People. Especially the ones who don't realise they're speaking.'

Tom stared. 'There's no one else up here.'

'There isn't,' Yusuf agreed. 'Not really.'

Tom didn't understand, and part of him didn't want to.

Yusuf pulled a cloth from his pack and handed it to him. 'For your head.'

The cotton smelt faintly of turmeric. He pressed it briefly to the wound, and it came away pink.

The sting made his eyes water, but it was a good kind of pain – proof he was still here.

When he lowered his hand, his watch caught his eye. The glass was cracked, a thin line splitting the face in two. The second hand had stopped dead.

'Eleven twenty-two,' he muttered.

Yusuf glanced down. 'Is that when you fell?'

Tom nodded. 'Must've been.'

He tried to twist the crown, but it was jammed solid.

'It's supposed to be shockproof,' he said. 'Guess they didn't mean this.'

He turned his wrist in the light. A bead of condensation sat under the glass, trapped like breath. 'It's strange,' he said quietly. 'You don't realise how much you rely on something until it stops working. I've had this thing for years. I check it without even thinking.'

Yusuf said nothing.

Tom gave a small, tired laugh. 'Now it's broken, I don't even know what time it is. Could be morning. Could be next week.'

'Maybe that's all right,' Yusuf said. 'You don't need to know what time it is to keep moving.'

Tom stared at the still hands. 'Feels like it stopped with me.'

'Maybe it's waiting for you,' Yusuf replied.

Tom let the watch drop back into his lap. He didn't answer, but for the first time since he'd fallen, he noticed the sound of water somewhere nearby – a faint drip, like the mountain was thawing.

'You were lucky,' Yusuf said, calmly. 'Ten feet more and the mountain would have kept you.'

Tom looked out past the ridge. Snow drifted sideways.

He wanted to ask who this man was. What he was doing here. But all that came out was:

'I didn't pack food.'

Yusuf didn't flinch. 'No?'

'I brought ... a spring onion,' Tom muttered.

That got a chuckle. 'A spring onion?'

'Don't ask.'

'I won't.'

Yusuf reached into his coat and pulled out a small tin. He prized it open and offered it to Tom.

Custard creams.

Tom took one and ate it slowly.

'Thanks,' he said quietly.

'You know,' Yusuf said after a pause, 'most people bring Kendal mint cake or trail mix.'

'Yeah, well,' Tom said with a half-smile. 'I panicked. Grabbed whatever was in the fridge.'

Yusuf nodded gravely, like he was considering it. 'A bold choice. One spring onion – nature's energy bar.'

'It's organic,' he said after a moment, deadpan.

Yusuf smiled. 'Then that's all right, then.'

They continued to sit in silence.

Not the kind of silence that demanded explanation. The kind that made space. The kind that didn't ask anything of you.

Yusuf's gaze stayed on the snow, not on Tom.

'You're not a climber,' Tom said eventually.

'No.'

'Not rescue.'

'No.'

'Then what are you?'

'I suppose,' Yusuf said, 'I'm what you needed.'

Tom didn't answer. He didn't know how.

His thoughts drifted. To Clare. To the note. To all the things he'd carried up the mountain.

'I meant to propose,' he said, voice raw.

'I know,' Yusuf replied.

Tom looked at him. 'You do?'

Yusuf just nodded.

'I waited too long. She didn't wait.'

'No one does.'

Tom closed his eyes.

'I thought climbing this might ... I don't know. Prove something.'

'Did it?'

'I'm not sure. Maybe. A little.'

Another silence.

Then: 'Do you believe in miracles?' Tom asked.

Yusuf's expression didn't change. 'I believe people don't always recognise them when they arrive.'

Snow began to fall softer.

'I've been holding on,' Tom said. 'To all the wrong things.'

Tom looked down at his lap. Snow gathered in the creases of his coat. His hands, raw and trembling, unzipped his coat and began to search the inside pockets. He wasn't sure why.

His fingers closed around paper, and he pulled out a crumpled receipt. The ink had smudged, but the words were still legible:

Blake's Coffee & Kitchen – Newcastle

2x Chai Latte

2x Orange Juice

1x Pink Slice

1x Flapjack

1x Salt & Vinegar Crisps

'We'd been visiting one of her uni friends. Long day, long drive back. She made us stop for snacks – crisps, a flapjack, and a pink slice she said looked too cheerful to leave behind.'

Tom smiled faintly.

'She called it "double drinks". One for joy, one for

hydration. I called it ridiculous.'

The receipt crackled between his fingers. 'She'd wiped cinnamon foam off my lip and made me promise to be less boring.'

He laid the receipt gently on his knee.

Next, he pulled out a small, smooth pebble. Painted with a now-faded love heart.

'Pembrokeshire coast,' he murmured. 'Picnic on the cliffs. Smoked mackerel pâté and a crusty baguette we tore with our hands.

'She painted this while I lay with my head in her lap and pretended not to fall asleep.'

He turned the pebble over slowly in his palm before setting it atop the receipt.

'She said everything leaves a mark. Even us. Even if we don't mean to.'

Yusuf didn't speak.

Next, Tom drew out a slip of paper so soft it nearly folded itself.

He opened it.

You will find peace in unlikely places.

'Fortune cookie,' Tom said. 'The night we moved into the flat. We ate takeaway on the floor. No furniture – just boxes and dreams. She read it out like it was some grand prophecy and stuck it to the bathroom mirror with a Post-it note.'

Suddenly remembering, he reached back inside his coat pocket and reclaimed the faded Post-it note. He unfolded it again carefully, but he didn't need to read it – he already knew what it said:

Keep going.

You've got this.

– C x

Tom looked down at the things he hadn't meant to carry but somehow had:

A receipt

A pebble

A fortune slip

A Post-it note

Yusuf nodded toward them, one by one.

'A moment of joy,' he said, nodding at the receipt.

'A moment of love,' towards the pebble.

'A moment of hope,' towards the fortune.

'And a moment of strength, even when you forgot you had it,' towards the Post-it note.

Tom swallowed. Then, almost too quietly to hear:

'I didn't want to die,' he said. 'I just didn't care if I did.'

Yusuf didn't speak.

Didn't offer reassurance.

'I didn't bring them on purpose,' Tom said.

'Most of what matters finds its way in without permission,' Yusuf replied.

'You still came up here,' Yusuf said after a moment. 'People don't climb mountains unless some part of them still wants to see what's on the other side.'

Tom gave a hollow laugh. 'I didn't even know what I was looking for.'

'Most people don't,' Yusuf said. 'They call it getting away, but really, they're trying to return. To something they lost, or someone they used to be.'

For a long time, neither of them spoke. The air was still, the snow now falling so softly it seemed to hesitate before touching the ground.

Then, from somewhere far below the ridge, came the faint sound of bells. Not clear, not certain – just a lonely chime carried on the wind, bending and fading like it wasn't sure it belonged up here.

Tom frowned. 'Do you hear that?'

Yusuf turned his head slightly, listening. 'What do you think it is?'

'Church bells, maybe,' Tom said. 'It's Christmas morning. Could be Wasdale.'

He paused, brow furrowed. 'Or maybe it's just in my head.'

'Maybe both,' Yusuf said.

Tom heard the bells again and closed his eyes for a moment, letting the sound settle. He could almost see it – a small stone church at the edge of a frozen village, roof white with snow. Someone down there would be pulling on the bell rope, gloved hands red from the cold, because it was what they did every year, even if no one came.

He remembered going to their local church with his mum when he still lived at home. She'd never called herself religious, but she said the carols made her 'feel Christmassy.' Every Christmas Eve they'd sit near the back, too warm in their coats, whispering about how long the vicar's sermon might be. He'd watch her face soften when the choir started 'Silent Night', and every time, she'd squeeze his hand just before the last verse.

He hadn't realised how much he missed that until now – the warmth, the shared silence, the strange comfort of singing words he didn't believe in, just to see her smile.

The wind shifted, carrying the bells a little closer

before they faded again into the snow.

'They sound ... different up here,' Tom said quietly.

Yusuf smiled faintly. 'Everything does when you've been too long in the noise.'

Tom nodded, eyes still on the white horizon. For the first time in months, he didn't want to fill the silence. He just listened. To the ghost of the bells, to the sigh of the wind, and to something small and steady inside him beginning to thaw.

And maybe that's what unsettled him most – that peace could exist even here, after everything.

'You think I belong here?' he said, not sure if he was asking Yusuf or the mountain itself.

Yusuf didn't answer straight away. He looked out across the slope, the valley hidden beneath folds of mist.

'My grandfather used to tell me a story,' he said after a moment. 'About a sailor whose compass was broken – not useless, just off. A fraction to the east.

'Every voyage he made, he thought he was following true north, but the needle always led him slightly astray.'

Tom listened, the snow whispering around them.

'At first, it drove the sailor mad,' Yusuf went on.

‘He’d end up in the wrong harbours, miss his destinations, and arrive days later than planned.

‘He kept trying to fix it – polishing the brass, tapping the glass, and even praying over it once.’ A faint smile. ‘But the compass never changed. It kept pointing its own way.’

‘So, what happened?’ Tom asked.

‘He gave up fighting it,’ Yusuf said. ‘He stopped chasing the routes on other people’s maps and started following where the needle wanted to go. He found islands no one had charted. Places no one believed existed. All because his compass was crooked.’

Tom looked down at the snow between his boots. ‘You’re saying I’m broken.’

‘I’m saying you’re heading somewhere no map could’ve planned,’ Yusuf replied. ‘Maybe the fault isn’t the thing to fix. Maybe it’s the thing that leads you home – just somewhere you hadn’t thought to look yet.’

The wind shifted then, brushing snow across their footprints like a hand smoothing a page.

Yusuf smiled. ‘I think you belong somewhere. This is just where you started remembering.’

‘Remembering what?’

‘That you’re still here,’ Yusuf said softly. ‘That the world hasn’t finished with you yet.’

Tom didn't reply. But something in him – small, quiet, and stubborn – stirred at the words, like a buried ember catching its first breath of air.

Tom picked up the receipt, folded it, and tucked it back into his coat pocket. The fortune followed. Now, not carried as weight, but as a reminder. The Post-it note, too, went back where it belonged. The pebble he kept in his hand for a while longer. Turned it once. Let its quiet weight speak to him.

'I don't need to throw them away,' he said. 'Just ... carry them differently.'

Yusuf nodded. 'Exactly.'

After a long silence, Tom spoke again.

Not to Yusuf exactly, but not to himself either. Just aloud. As if the mountain needed to hear it.

'There's more,' he said. 'Things I never said. Things I should have.'

He let them come, one by one.

'I loved the way you greeted animals like they were old friends. Foxes, pigeons, and dogs tied outside shops. You spoke to all of them like you'd just run into them at a party.'

'I never told you how stubbornly loyal I thought it was that you only drank "biscuit tea". I always made sure we had some in.'

'You called Baileys "Christmas milk". Even in April. Especially in April.'

'I used to ring your phone when I knew it was off just to hear your cheery voicemail greeting.'

'You always ordered for me in restaurants. I loved feeling like you were looking after me.'

'You got genuinely excited every time you saw hollyhocks. Once you dragged me across a roundabout just to get a closer look. I didn't get it. But I do now.'

'You always ordered "double drinks". You said one was for hydration and one was for joy. You called it "balance".'

'If you liked a dress, you bought two. One for now, one for when the first got tired. You called it "future joy". I rolled my eyes. I was wrong.'

Tom paused. 'You made boring feel beautiful.'

The wind passed gently over them.

'I didn't tell you any of that,' he whispered. 'Not properly. I thought I had more time.'

Yusuf's reply came gently. 'It's not too late.'

Tom shook his head. 'It feels like it is.'

'Then carry them,' Yusuf said. 'Not as weight. As warmth.'

Tom didn't speak. But the storm inside him stilled.

After a while, Yusuf shifted slightly, brushing frost from his knee. 'There's a story,' he said. 'One my mother used to tell me.'

Tom glanced at him. 'Yeah?'

Yusuf nodded. 'About a man who carried a cracked pot. Every day, he'd walk to the well and fill it, then carry it back across the fields to his home. But by the time he arrived, the pot had leaked out half its water. It embarrassed him. He felt like a failure.'

He looked out at the snow-covered valley. 'But one spring, he noticed something different. On the side of the path where he always walked with the cracked pot, wildflowers had bloomed. Only that side. Every colour. Every shape. They followed the line of the leak like a secret garden. Because what he thought was broken had been watering something all along.'

Tom swallowed.

Yusuf didn't look at him. He just added, 'We don't always get to know what our pain grows. Not straight away. But it doesn't mean it grows nothing.'

Yusuf was quiet for a while. Then, softly:

'I think you've left more flowers than you realise.'

Tom stared at the snow.

It hadn't stopped hurting. It never would. But there was a lightness to it now.

He realised he'd spent months trying to outrun the pain when all it had wanted was to be seen. It wasn't the mountain that had broken him – it was the climb to avoid feeling anything at all. He'd filled the silence with noise – work, screens, half-hearted laughter – anything that kept him moving fast enough not to notice the ache. But grief, he understood now, didn't live in the moments you escaped. It waited patiently, like weather on the horizon, until you finally stopped running long enough to let it catch you. And here it was – not as a punishment, but as proof he'd once loved something worth losing.

He didn't feel better. But he didn't feel entirely broken either.

Not in this moment.

And for the first time, that felt like enough.

'When you're ready,' Yusuf said softly, 'I'll walk with you a while.'

Tom asked, 'Where?'

'Down's a start,' Yusuf replied.

CHAPTER FIVE
THE DESCENT

The snow softened underfoot, but the wind hadn't given up entirely. Tom's leg ached with every step. The dull, lingering kind that reminded him of every misstep and every ounce of effort it had taken to get up the mountain and now to come back down.

But he kept moving.

Yusuf walked ahead. He always seemed to find the right place to put his feet. Even when the path disappeared beneath drifts, Yusuf walked as if the mountain told him where to go.

Tom followed.

The red bobble on Yusuf's hat bounced gently with each step. Tom found comfort in it, like a heartbeat you could trust.

They walked in silence for a long time. Only the crunch of boots and the howl of the wind broke the stillness. The clouds above were beginning to fray, torn apart by unseen hands.

There was a peace in the silence, but it unnerved him. He wasn't used to this kind of quiet – not the absence of noise, but the absence of needing to *say* something. With Clare, he'd always filled the gaps. Banter, plans, logistics. Even in the car on holidays, he couldn't bear the silence for long. He'd fiddle with the radio, ask what she wanted for dinner, and suggest pit stops they didn't need. And now, walking behind Yusuf, he realised he didn't know how to be with someone without narrating it. But Yusuf didn't ask for anything. He just walked.

Tom let himself try.

The wind softened, but Tom's thoughts hadn't. Every step jarred something loose inside him – grief, guilt, regret.

Tom adjusted his sleeve, and for the first time since the fall, the cracked watch on his wrist caught the light. He glanced down out of habit and froze. The second hand had moved, a faint tremor beneath the cracked glass, as if the watch had simply been waiting for him to notice. Just one small, jerky tick. Then another.

The glass was still fractured, the face still scarred, but it was working again.

'Look at that,' he murmured.

Yusuf turned. 'What is it?'

'It's ticking.' Tom held out his wrist, half in disbelief. 'It stopped when I fell. Eleven twenty-two. I thought it was done.'

Yusuf studied it for a moment, then smiled faintly. 'Maybe it just needed time.'

Tom gave a quiet laugh through his breath. 'That's poetic.'

'Or practical,' Yusuf said. 'Sometimes things start again when you do.'

Tom didn't answer, but he didn't look away either. The faint motion of the second hand was hypnotic – steady, imperfect, alive. He let his sleeve fall back into place and kept walking.

The wind shifted again. It was now barely a whisper. Snowflakes drifted gently. Tom blinked against the white blur, and, for a heartbeat, someone else was walking beside him. Someone very slim. Their hood up. Their stride light and familiar, like they were just out for a wintry walk. Clare. Not *ghostly*. But there, like a memory had stumbled into the present. He didn't say anything. Just stared. When he blinked again, it was only Yusuf. A few steps ahead as he always had been. Tom shook his head and kept walking. He didn't believe in ghosts. But whatever walked beside him just then, he didn't question.

Some memories didn't haunt. They just held your hand for a while.

It made him wonder if healing wasn't forgetting but learning how to walk beside the memory without needing it to go away.

They followed the curve of the ridge, where the snow had drifted thick against the rocks. Tom's boot caught on something half buried, and he stopped. A flash of dull metal broke through the white. He crouched and brushed at it until the outline appeared – a thermos flask, dented and rusted at the edges. The lid was cracked, and a crust of frozen coffee clung to the rim. Someone had dropped it long ago.

He turned it over in his hands.

Scratched faintly into the side were three letters: *CES*.

'Someone else came this way,' Tom said quietly.

Yusuf looked over his shoulder. 'They always do.'

'Think they made it down?'

Yusuf didn't answer straight away. He brushed snow from a nearby stone and crouched beside him.

'Maybe. Maybe not. But the fact it's here means they carried something warm for a while.'

Tom nodded, thumb tracing the initials. The metal was ice-cold, but for a moment, it felt like holding someone else's story. He set it gently back where he'd found it. Maybe it was nothing, or maybe someone had once needed that warmth as badly as he had. Either way, it felt wrong to move it – like disturbing a story that wasn't his to finish.

As they walked on, Tom found himself glancing back once. The thermos sat half swallowed by snow again, waiting for spring.

They rounded a bend where a dry-stone wall slumped beneath the weight of winter. That's when Tom saw it – a sheep, half buried in snow, and struggling to move. Its legs kicked aimlessly, weak and trembling.

He paused.

But Yusuf moved without hesitation. He crouched beside the animal, calm as ever, brushing the snow gently from its back. No fuss. No words. He slipped an arm beneath its belly and lifted with quiet strength. The sheep stumbled upright and stood blinking for a moment before wandering off into the whiteness. Yusuf didn't watch it long. He simply turned, nodded once, and kept walking.

Tom hadn't moved. Just stood there, hands in useless fists, while Yusuf hadn't hesitated.

Tom had always been the one with the map. The checklist. The plan to fix whatever was broken. But now, watching the sheep vanish into the snow, he felt like a child.

Tom stumbled slightly as they resumed, his boot sliding on a hidden patch of ice.

The slip brought him to a stop just long enough to notice movement ahead. A flicker of red against the white.

A robin had landed on a half-buried post, chest bright as embers, and its feathers fluffed against the cold. It hopped once, tilting its head, as if unbothered by the storm or the two figures in its path.

Tom smiled faintly. 'Clare used to say robins meant someone was thinking of you.'

Yusuf didn't speak for a moment. The wind had gone still again, as if listening too.

'Do you believe that?' he asked finally.

Tom's breath clouded in the air. 'I didn't. Not really. But I think I do now.'

The robin gave a small shake, sending a dust of snow into the air, then took off. A streak of red vanished into the white.

Tom watched until it disappeared. 'You wait for a sign, and when it comes, it's smaller than you think.'

'Small things are easier to carry,' Yusuf said.

Tom nodded, still watching the space where it had been, then adjusted his pack and followed on for a few steps before his ankle twisted, just enough to sting. He hissed under his breath, the noise half pain, half exhaustion.

Yusuf didn't turn. Just slowed his pace enough to keep them together.

Tom swore softly, and not at the pain. He hated how fragile he felt. Like a man cracked open by weather and silence.

A memory surfaced – one Tom hadn't thought about in months.

'Not everything needs fixing, Tom,' Clare had said once, when he'd clattered around the kitchen, offering solutions she hadn't asked for.

'Sometimes you just sit with someone. That's it.'

Back then, he'd rolled his eyes.

But watching Yusuf lift a sheep from the snow without a word, Clare's words landed differently now.

Maybe she hadn't meant 'do nothing'.

Maybe she meant 'be there'.

He used to think love was doing things. Fixing things. Making things work. But maybe love sometimes meant being still. Being present. Even when there was nothing to fix.

Tom's fingers no longer trembled. His breath still came hard, but it didn't hurt anymore.

'I thought I came up here to be alone,' he said

eventually.

Yusuf didn't turn. 'Maybe you did.'

'But I wasn't.'

'No,' Yusuf said softly. 'You weren't.'

The path sloped downward. They passed a ridge where the snow had been carved by wind into delicate, wind-blown sculptures. The kind of beauty you only see if you're really looking.

Tom slowed, almost without meaning to, drawn by the quiet elegance of it, as if the mountain itself was reminding him that beauty could survive even after the storm.

He let his eyes follow the shapes, unhurried, as if the mountain were offering something only visible when you were paying attention.

When was the last time he'd really looked at anything? Not through the lens of a task or a problem to solve, but simply to witness it. To be with it. Not Clare. Not himself. Not even the world. He had spent so long trying to fix everything that he'd forgotten what it meant to notice.

But now he saw.

The snow didn't need him.

The mountain made no demands.

It just was.

And, for the first time in a long while, so was he.

Tom felt something change in his chest, like a hand unclenching.

He asked, 'How did you find me?'

'You called out.'

'I didn't.'

'Not with your mouth.'

Tom didn't reply. He didn't need to. A part of him understood exactly what Yusuf meant.

They paused near a flat ledge where the world opened beneath them in layers as the mist slowly lifted. The air had that strange, crisp brightness that comes after snowfall, like it was new.

Tom sat on a boulder, catching his breath. Yusuf crouched beside him and opened a small tin. From a foil wrapper, Yusuf broke off a piece of dark chocolate and held it out. Tom accepted it without a word.

The bitterness came first. Then something softer. It lingered on his tongue like a memory.

They used to go to that little coffee shop near the old windmill. The one with mismatched cups. Clare loved it, even though the coffee was average and the service was always slow.

Every time, they served a wafer of dark chocolate on the saucer. She never ate hers. Just smiled, slid it over to his side of the table, and said, 'You're the one with the sweet tooth.'

It was a tiny thing. Insignificant.

But he couldn't remember the last time anyone had given him something small like that. And maybe that's why it was easier to keep pretending he didn't need anything.

He hadn't thought about that place in months. The way Clare slid the chocolate across the saucer without looking at him.

It wasn't about the chocolate. It never had been.

'I used to think being strong meant never needing help,' Tom said.

Yusuf tilted his head, listening.

'But now I think strength is admitting when you're lost. Or hurt. Or scared.'

His throat tightened. For a second, he could no longer find the words. He just stood there, snow settling in his hair, feeling like something inside him had been exposed.

Yusuf nodded once. 'There's a story,' he said,

'about a traveller in the desert. He asks God, "Why is the path so long?" And God replies, "Because you haven't arrived yet."'

Tom let out a breath. 'That's it, isn't it? We all think we're supposed to have arrived already.'

He'd lost count of the times he'd whispered, 'I should be better by now,' as if saying it might make it true.

But maybe the path wasn't broken. Maybe he just hadn't arrived yet.

'But we're still walking.'

Tom smiled faintly.

'Still walking,' he echoed.

They paused at the curve of the path, where meltwater had collected in a thin pool edged with ice. The wind had eased now, and for the first time all day the air felt still enough to hold its own silence. The pool mirrored the pale sky above it – washed-out blue veiled with moving white – and for a moment, Tom caught sight of himself in the water.

He hardly recognised the man looking back.

The face was drawn and pale, but the eyes – his eyes – seemed different. Calmer. The constant tension that had lived there for months had loosened its grip.

He crouched closer. The surface trembled, distorting the reflection until it no longer looked like him at all, just a shape caught between past and present.

A drop of meltwater fell from a branch above and sent ripples across the surface. When the image settled again, he wasn't alone.

There, beside his own reflection, was the faintest suggestion of another figure – a dark coat, the shadow of a red woollen hat, just enough to make him catch his breath.

'Yusuf?' he said quietly.

But when he turned, Yusuf was a few paces behind him, hands in his pockets, watching. The reflection lingered a second longer, then broke apart with the wind.

Tom's chest tightened, but not from fear. There was something comforting about it.

He crouched lower, resting his palms on his knees.

He thought of all the times he'd seen himself before now. In mirrors, in shop windows, on video calls. And he hated the sight. The hollow cheeks, the tired eyes, the sense of being a stranger in his own skin. But this time, as he looked, he didn't flinch.

This time, he looked long enough to recognise himself again.

'I used to avoid mirrors,' he murmured. 'Couldn't stand what looked back.'

Yusuf didn't reply. He didn't need to.

A breeze passed, gentle and cool, and the reflection scattered completely, light breaking across the surface. Beneath it, Tom saw the dark shape of stone.

He straightened slowly, feeling the ache in his knees. He stepped across the puddle carefully, his boot breaking the surface with a soft splash. Ripples spread outward, catching the light before fading.

They walked a little further in silence. The snow underfoot was softer now, but the ache in his chest had returned. It was different this time.

'There were nights I hoped the pain would just stop,' he said. 'That I'd close my eyes and not open them again.'

He didn't look at Yusuf when he added, 'But I never wanted to die. I just didn't know how to live anymore.'

Yusuf didn't answer straight away. He just kept walking, the crunch of his boots marking time.

Yusuf spoke softly, eyes on the snow ahead. 'A man once asked God why He was silent during the worst moments of his life. And God said, "I was there. But you didn't recognise My footsteps because they looked like your own."'

Tom closed his eyes for a moment. He could hear his heartbeat. It no longer raced. It had become a quiet, steady metronome.

The descent continued. They moved slowly, passing through shifting light and dissolving mist. The trees below grew closer. They were real now. Not just shapes in the distance. The valley was no longer a concept. It was land. Earth. Home.

'I used to think faith meant certainty,' Tom said as they walked. 'Like you had to *know* something to believe it.'

'And now?'

'I think maybe it's the opposite. Maybe it's the not-knowing. But walking anyway.'

Yusuf's eyes twinkled. 'Then you're already there.'

Tom laughed gently. 'I don't feel there.'

'No one ever does,' Yusuf said. 'Not until they look back and realise they kept going.'

They followed the curve of the ridge, where the path narrowed to a ledge no wider than a boot. The wind picked up again. It was not fierce, but enough to steal their breath. Yusuf was a few paces ahead.

Tom tried to call out to him. 'Yusuf!'

The sound was whipped away instantly, swallowed by the emptiness. But then, half a second later, it came back – faint, warped, but still his voice. It echoed once, then again, bouncing between the cliffs like the mountain was repeating it to itself.

Tom stopped. For a moment, he could almost believe there were two of them calling out across the white.

He tried again, quieter this time. 'Yusuf.'

The same reply – a thin echo, softer now, fading into the snow.

Tom exhaled a shaky breath that might have been a laugh. 'Guess it's just me,' he said.

Yusuf turned slightly, not quite smiling. 'It always was. But that doesn't mean you were alone.'

The wind eased again, the air still ringing faintly with the sound of his own voice as if it lingered, waiting for him to catch up to it.

They passed a crooked signpost half buried in snow. Beyond it, the trees thinned, and the car park came into view.

Tom's car sat where he'd left it.

A sharp caw echoed from the trees. Tom jumped. When he turned back, Yusuf was gone.

Tom froze.

He spun in place, scanning the path. There was nowhere to hide, just the smooth slope of snow behind him.

He looked down.

Only one set of footprints.

His own.

His breath caught.

He called, 'Yusuf?'

Nothing.

Just the hush of the mountain and the whisper of wind in the trees.

But there was warmth, too. A quietness that wasn't emptiness. Something he could carry.

He stared at the space Yusuf had been and found

himself smiling a little.

Maybe Yusuf had never really been *beside* him. Maybe he'd been *within* him. Or maybe, for a time, they'd simply walked the same path.

Tom touched the inside of his coat where the receipt, the pebble, the fortune slip, and the Post-it note still rested.

He hadn't let go. But the weight had changed.

He took one more look at the mountain. Then he whispered, 'Thank you.'

He made his way toward the car.

And for the first time in a long while – longer than he could measure – Tom Briggs walked not to escape something behind, but toward something ahead.

Something like hope.

CHAPTER SIX
THE COAT HE LEFT BEHIND

The path had led him back to the car, as if the mountain had finished with him.

There it was. Dirty. Familiar. Slightly pathetic. But it hadn't left. The old Peugeot looked like it had been waiting for him with a kind of loyalty that bordered on pity. Its headlights, fogged with age, seemed to squint through the snowfall like tired eyes. It wasn't much, but it was his. The only thing in his life that hadn't left when it could.

Snow had gathered in the wheel arches and along the wipers, softening its edges until it looked almost harmless. The kind of car that blended in everywhere, that no one ever really saw. Much like him, he thought.

He approached it slowly, half expecting it to vanish the closer he got. He pressed a hand to the bonnet, unsure what he was hoping to feel. Warmth, maybe. Proof of presence. But it was cold. Lifeless.

He didn't get in straight away. He stood for a moment beside the driver's door, the key cold in his hand, staring up at the mountain. The wind had dropped. Only the faint hiss of falling snow remained.

For the first time that day, the silence didn't feel like punishment. Just space. A space big enough to hold whatever came next.

He stood there a little longer, the mountain behind him fading into the dusk.

The world seemed smaller now. Quieter.

The snow creaked softly under his boots. He brushed a layer from the mirror and saw his own face looking back – hollow-eyed, lips split from the cold – and realised how long it had been since he'd really looked at himself. Not the version in video calls or shop windows, but the one that still flinched at memories. The one who had loved and lost and somehow kept breathing anyway.

Eventually, he climbed inside. The engine stayed off. The silence felt different now – not empty, just still.

He sat there with his hands on the steering wheel,

breathing slowly, feeling the ache of the day settle into something almost peaceful.

Her scrunchie was still looped around the gearstick from some long-forgotten road trip, sun-faded and stretched. He'd never taken it off. Couldn't. It had become part of the car, part of the ritual – check the doors, adjust the seat, check the mirrors, glance at the scrunchie.

His breath misted the air, rising and vanishing before it reached the windscreen. For a strange second, he wished he could disappear that easily – dissolve, reform, come back as something simpler. Maybe water. Maybe light. Something that didn't have to decide what came next.

The windscreen fogged over completely. Out of habit, he wiped a circle clear with his sleeve. This time, it cleared easily – no smears, no resistance – revealing the soft white world outside.

The snow was falling heavier now, each flake melting the moment it touched the glass. It looked like the world was erasing itself and starting over.

For a moment, he caught his reflection in the mirror again. Tired. Pale. But alive. And just beside him, faint and flickering, the blur of a red woollen hat.

He blinked, and it was gone.

Tom smiled faintly.

The key turned with a judder. The Peugeot coughed, complained, then wheezed into life. The heater gave a tired moan, pushing out air that smelt of damp and long-forgotten mints.

The radio flickered on mid-song – the same Christmas hymn that had grated on him hours before.

The words drifted softly this time, the melody fragile against the static. He remembered Clare humming it one December, sleeves dusted with flour as she rolled pastry in their kitchen to make shortbread reindeer.

He hadn't listened to the hymn since. But now, it sounded different – not an anthem of loss.

This time, he didn't turn it off.

He let it play.

For a long time, he didn't move. He just sat with his hands on the wheel, the engine idling, and his eyes fixed on the glovebox.

Eventually, he reached across and opened it. The spring onion was still there. Bent. Slightly shrivelled. It looked like it had tried to keep going, even in the dark. He couldn't decide if that made him feel hopeful or worse.

He could almost hear Clare laughing at him for

holding onto things that didn't make any sense. Like the five IKEA Allen keys from when they bought furniture, the faded festival wristband he never took off, or the half-drunk bottle of Diet Coke in his cupboard he swore he'd finish someday.

'You and your ridiculous little things,' she'd tease, always with a smile.

It wasn't just a spring onion, though. Not to him. It was an attempt at holding on to something. Something alive. Something to take care of. A way of saying, 'I'm still here.'

With a soft sigh, he put it in his pocket.

'Maybe I should get a plant next time,' he thought.

He put the car in gear and drove. Back down the narrow lane. Past ice-crusted stone walls and skeletal trees. The roads were darker now, and the sky was already bruised by Christmas night.

A growl in his stomach reminded him of how hungry he was. The car, like him, was running on fumes; the fuel gauge hovered just above empty.

Clare would've hated that.

She used to top up the tank the minute it dipped below half.

If the needle hovered near the red, she'd suck in a breath through her teeth and give him *that* look.

'Stop playing the petrol game,' she'd mutter, eyes glued to the gauge like it was a countdown clock.

He used to laugh it off. Called it her 'petrol panic'.

But she wasn't joking.

'You like flirting with empty,' she'd say. 'I like knowing I'll make it home.'

He blinked at the dashboard light. It was glowing now – a soft orange warning.

She would've pulled over.

So he drove to the first petrol station he found and did just that.

The forecourt was empty. One overhead light flickered with a tired buzz. Inside, a teenager stood behind the till with headphones in, chewing something without interest. The slogan on her T-shirt read *Allergic to People,* as if she needed a warning label. The letters were cracked and faded, suggesting it had been true for a while.

Behind her, a small TV balanced on a stack of cardboard boxes played the *Gavin and Stacey* 'Christmas Special' on low volume – the one where Nessa and Smithy exchange presents in the car park. The sound was tinny and distorted, but Tom caught fragments – canned laughter, a burst of the theme tune, and someone shouting, 'Oh, what's occurring?' The teenager didn't look up.

For a heartbeat, he thought how strange it was – to stand in a fluorescent forecourt on Christmas night, while other people in other rooms laughed at something they already knew by heart. The world kept spinning, even when you weren't in it.

Tom wandered the aisles, each footstep echoing off the tiles. The shelves offered very little – tinned soup, crisps, a few dented tins of beans, and a pot of basil pesto pasta, the label promising *fresh taste,* though the smell hinted at something far less optimistic.

Nothing felt quite right.

Until he saw it.

A single Pot Noodle. Original Curry. The label slightly torn. The shelf beneath it empty.

It didn't feel like a choice. It felt like fate. It felt like the universe had stripped everything back to the truth – him, alone, on Christmas night, with a meal that didn't pretend to be anything it wasn't.

He bought it, gave a polite nod the teenager hadn't earned, and stepped back into the cold. She'd looked at the gash on his head with a faint frown, like she was trying to remember if head injuries were part of some policy she hadn't read properly. Then, she blinked, said nothing, and went back to chewing.

Tom stood outside, holding the Pot Noodle like a question. Unopened. Pointless without hot water.

He considered going back in. Asking her for a kettle. But he already knew how that would go. She hadn't looked up when he paid. Hadn't spoken. Had barely seemed real.

No – she wouldn't help. It was Christmas night, and she clearly didn't want to be working. And, Christmas or not, this wasn't her problem. People were meant to show up, pay, and leave. Not ask for favours. And certainly not from her.

He returned to his car and paused.

Across the road, half-hidden behind a hedge, was a building he hadn't noticed before. He scanned the road behind him. No sign. No marker. Nothing to explain how he'd missed it.

It wasn't grand or showy. Just a small, sturdy building that looked like it knew how to keep secrets and stay warm in winter. A green door sat beneath a porch strung with fairy lights, one or two flickering in protest. Above it, a wooden sign swayed gently on iron chains, the hand-painted letters reading, *The Loft*. The paint was chipped in places, but the name still stood proud. It looked like the sort of place walkers stumbled into by accident and returned to year after year.

He was surprised he'd missed it.

Maybe it hadn't been there before.

Or maybe, like so many things lately, he just hadn't been paying attention.

He crossed the road and approached the door.

The handle turned before he could even knock.

'Come in, love,' said the woman standing in the doorway. 'You look half-frozen.'

She had silver hair piled into something that might once have been a twist but now looked more like a startled bird's nest, pinned in place with what appeared to be a teaspoon. Her lipstick had made a bid for freedom, smeared just slightly beyond the natural borders of her lips, like she'd applied it in a moving vehicle. A knitted red cardigan hung from her shoulders, studded with mismatched buttons. One of her slippers was blue. The other was a Wellington boot. Behind her smudged glasses, her eyes sparkled.

She motioned for him to enter, nearly upsetting an umbrella stand with the enthusiasm of it. 'In you pop. Careful of the hedgehog on the doorstep! He's only plastic, but I'm told he bruises easily!'

'I just...' Tom held up the Pot Noodle like it was evidence. 'I was wondering if I could borrow some hot water.'

She squinted at it. 'Classy Christmas dinner,' she said.

'It's become a tradition,' he replied, more deadpan than humorous.

She smiled anyway and stepped aside. 'I've got the kettle on. Come in.'

The inside smelt of pine disinfectant and toast. There was a radio playing something soft and wordless in the background.

As Tom followed the woman through the narrow hallway, he noticed a collection of framed photographs on the wall. Walkers in waterproofs, mugs of tea raised to the camera, and snow-swept peaks behind them. A few were sun-faded and one was slightly crooked. In the corner of a frame, a blur of red caught his eye – a hat, maybe, or a trick of the light.

The radio shifted, static flickering, and the faint notes of a Christmas hymn filled the space – the same one that had played in his car. Jackie hummed along without seeming to notice, her voice light and tuneless, but somehow comforting.

The photographs watched them pass, a gallery of strangers and half-remembered winters. In one frame, the snow blurred the horizon into a white silence so complete it looked almost painted. Tom wondered if it was this mountain. If it was today.

'I'm Jackie,' she said as she got to the kitchen.

'Tom.'

'You want a cuppa too, Tom?'

He hesitated, then nodded. 'Yeah. That'd be great.'

Tom lingered in the doorway while Jackie disappeared into the kitchen, her voice trailing off somewhere.

He wasn't sure what kind of place this was – a guesthouse, a refuge, or something stranger – but for the first time that day, he didn't feel like he had to explain himself to anyone.

When Jackie's voice called out, 'Milk or sugar, love?' he startled slightly, then cleared his throat.

'Milk, please,' he said. 'Oat if you've got it.'

'Coming right up,' she replied, her tone brisk and

bright. 'And don't worry, I don't judge a man for instant noodles. We've all been there.'

Tom stepped just inside the threshold, not wanting to drag half the mountain in with him. On a side table, a plant drooped in a chipped mug that read *World's Okayest Cook*. Beside it sat a snow globe whose water had turned the colour of weak tea. Nearby, a pair of walking boots waited by the radiator, one upright, one slouched as though too tired to keep pretending.

He hadn't realised how long it had been since he'd seen a room that felt lived in – cluttered, warm, and unapologetically human. His own flat had grown too quiet, too tidy, as though it were waiting for someone else to come back.

Jackie came to the doorway a few minutes later with two steaming mugs of tea and his rehydrating Pot Noodle balanced on a tray.

'You look like someone who's had a day,' she said.

Tom smiled faintly, taking the mug of tea. 'Yeah. I climbed Scafell Pike.'

She raised her eyebrows. 'On Christmas Day?'

'I'm not great at timing.'

She laughed, the kind of laugh that warmed you without trying to. 'Clearly. You on your own?'

He nodded.

'Sort of,' he said. A shrug followed. 'Mostly.'

Jackie had set the tray down on a small table between two armchairs in the hallway, the fabric worn to softness.

They sat in companionable silence for a few minutes, broken only by the quiet slurp of noodles.

'You're welcome to stay,' she said eventually. 'We've got a few rooms free. No pressure.'

Tom hesitated. He was still soaked to the skin beneath his coat.

'All right,' he said. 'Just the one night.'

'Fifteen quid, if you don't mind making your own breakfast.'

'I think I can manage that.'

Jackie gathered the empty mugs.

'I'll wash these in the morning,' she said, though she was already halfway to the sink.

'It's always quieter on Christmas night. Just me, the radio, and whoever the mountain sends down.'

Tom smiled faintly. 'Does that happen often?'

'Oh, you'd be surprised.'

She nodded towards a pinboard near the door, its cork faded. Photographs covered almost every inch – walkers grinning in waterproofs, families with rucksacks, a pair of cyclists holding up a punctured tyre like a trophy.

'Every one of them turned up by accident,' she said. 'Broken boots, broken hearts, you name it. Some came back, some didn't.'

Tom stepped closer. The photos were all slightly yellowed. Near the bottom, one picture caught his eye – a picture of a man standing by a wooden stile, hood pulled up against the rain. His face was half in shadow, but his stance – calm, a little awkward – felt oddly familiar. A red bobble hat hung from his hand.

Jackie followed his gaze.

'That one was years ago. Funny fellow. Always asked if he could help with things – fixing the boiler, chopping wood, that sort. Never told me his name.'

She tapped the photo lightly, then looked at Tom.

'Kind eyes, though. Like yours. You meet people like that and think you'll remember them forever. Then one day you realise you can't even remember their voice.'

She said it lightly, but something thoughtful passed behind her glasses. Then she smiled again, briskly, as if turning a page.

'Right, enough of my rambling. You'll be needing your sleep.'

He smiled. 'Thank you for the tea.'

'Tea fixes most things,' she said. 'The rest usually sort themselves out if you give them half a chance.'

She handed him a key, then paused, noticing how wet his sleeves were.

'You'll want dry clothes. We've got a lost property box in the laundry room. Feel free to take something.'

Tom thanked her and made his way to the small room off the hallway.

A cracked plastic bin sat beneath a handwritten sign that just said *LOST* in faded Sharpie.

He rummaged through the lost property bin. Mostly odd gloves, ancient fleeces, and the occasional single sock. Then his hand brushed something heavier.

A navy coat.

He lifted it out slowly and turned it over.

On the lapel, pinned just above the pocket, was a small silver swallow. Its wings stretched wide.

Tom stared at it for a long time.

'Find anything?' Jackie's voice floated in from the hallway.

He stepped into the doorway, holding the coat like an artefact. 'Where did this come from?'

Jackie squinted at it. 'That one? Hmm.' She scratched her temple before adjusting her glasses. 'You know, I'm not entirely sure.'

Tom raised an eyebrow.

'I *think* it was left a few years ago. Man stayed over Christmas. Didn't say much, but his eyes were kind.'

She paused.

'Or maybe that was someone else.'

She smiled faintly.

'I've got a bit of a habit of taking in stray coats. And stray stories. And sometimes stray people.'

She looked at the swallow pin and tilted her head. 'Beautiful, isn't it? Always meant to give it to the charity shop, but I didn't. Don't know why.' Her voice softened. 'Guess I hoped someone might need it.'

Jackie stayed where she was, watching him for a moment over the rims of her glasses. 'Funny thing about coats,' she said. 'You never really know whose stories are still caught in the lining. People forget how much they leave behind in pockets.'

Tom traced the edge of the swallow pin with his thumb. 'Maybe some things are meant to be found again,' he said quietly.

'Maybe.' Her smile deepened. Not wide but knowing.

'Either way, it looks like that one's yours now. Things have a way of choosing where they belong.'

Before he could ask more, Jackie gave a small

shrug, as though brushing away something unspoken.

'You'd be surprised how many coats never get claimed.'

Tom wasn't sure what to say.

He wasn't even sure what Jackie had meant; it was as if she wasn't speaking literally.

He just nodded, the coat still folded in his arms, and headed upstairs.

His room was small but warm. A thick blanket was folded at the foot of the bed. The carpet was worn but clean. It wasn't the kind of place you planned to end up, but it was enough for tonight.

The air carried the faint, unmistakable scent of *Midnight Blooms* Zoflora – that floral sweetness that always clung to Clare's cleaning cloths. She loved the smell of it. He could picture her now, moving through their old flat with a spray bottle in one hand, humming without realising, and pausing every so often to admire her work with a small, satisfied smile.

She'd always been like that – constantly cleaning, polishing, and straightening cushions that didn't need it.

Even mowing the lawn in dresses that really weren't made for it, the hem catching on the grass, hair pinned up and sunglasses sliding down her nose. Probably something from Vinted. She swore by Vinted. Every parcel felt like a victory, a bargain rescued from landfill.

In 2022, she'd made it her personal challenge – 'Nothing new in '22'. Not clothes, not furniture, not even books. Only second-hand things, in her quiet bid to help save the planet. She'd said it with a grin the first time, half joking, then stuck to it more fiercely than most people kept resolutions.

He could almost hear her voice drifting through the open door, half laughing as she called out for him to come and see what a fiver could buy these days. The memory didn't ache anymore. It just settled beside him.

Tom set the spring onion gently on the bedside table, like a strange green keepsake.

Then, he put the coat on.

It fit perfectly.

He sat down slowly, the fabric settling around him like memory. The radiator ticked in the corner. Somewhere down the hall, someone laughed.

His phone buzzed.

A message from his mum:

No pressure, love. But we've booked the usual

table at the Taj Mahal for Boxing Day, 7pm. Come if you feel up to it. First poppadom's yours. x

He stared at the screen.

That restaurant. Paneer jalfrezi. Chilli naan. Bombay potatoes. His dad complaining about the lager prices and ordering two anyway. It was their tradition.

Solitude had crept in so slowly he hadn't noticed it taking root. Days blurred into one another. Conversations got shorter. Texts went unanswered. People had stopped inviting him to things. Not unkindly, but gently, as if assuming he'd say no. And eventually, he had.

Which was why the message from his mum had landed differently. Not a guilt trip. Not a plea. Just: 'First poppadom's yours.'

No expectations. No pressure. Just a place at the table waiting quietly for him to claim it. And somehow, that made him feel more seen than anything else ever could.

He typed:

Thanks, Mum. I'll be there. x

He hovered for a second. Then pressed send.

The phone went dark in his palm. He placed it beside the spring onion and lay back on the bed in the jacket that might not have been Yusuf's or might have been exactly that.

He didn't know.

Outside, sleet began to tap gently against the window. It was light and irregular, like quiet applause. He listened to it build and fade, a rhythm without expectation, as if the night itself approved of small steps forward.

He thought of the footprints in the snow. Of warmth shared in silence. Of the coat with the silver swallow and the taste of chocolate that lingered longer than expected.

Maybe Yusuf had been real. Maybe not.

Maybe it didn't matter.

Something had changed.

And whatever had walked beside him – real or not – had helped him find his way down.

And for the first time in a long while, he wasn't afraid of the way back up.

CHAPTER SEVEN
THE ADDRESS

Light spilt in through the attic window like it had a hangover and was now fumbling its way across the floorboards. It reached the side of the bed and touched Tom's face.

He stirred.

The light pressed against his eyelids, insistent and uninvited, and nudged him into motion.

The bedsheets were coarse but clean. The kind that felt like they'd been dried on a line in real air and not tumbled to death in a machine. They clung gently to his skin, still holding the faint warmth of sleep.

A crocheted blanket had slipped halfway down

during the night. As he moved, the fibres caught on his toes. It was scratchy but not unpleasant.

The pillow beneath his head carried the faint scent of someone else's fabric softener – lavender, maybe, or something vaguely floral that didn't belong to him. It was unfamiliar but oddly comforting, like staying in a distant relative's house as a child. Safe, but not your own. The scent reminded him that he was somewhere different.

And yet, he didn't feel the urge to move. Not yet. It was like the room itself was asking him to stay a little longer.

Eventually, he swung his legs over the edge of the bed and yawned. His feet met the cold floorboards, and he flinched slightly at the shock of it. The boards creaked in protest, as if surprised to be needed so early. He blinked.

He sat with his elbows on his knees, his head in his hands, and not quite ready to face the day. He ran a hand through his hair, more out of ritual than necessity, and stared at nothing in particular.

He thought about all the hotel rooms they'd ever stayed in – European city breaks, weddings, and all those last-minute coastal escapes when life got too heavy and they just needed sea air and each other. No matter how short the stay, Clare would always make the bed before they left. Even if it had already been tidied once. Even if they'd only popped in for a few hours' rest. She'd smooth the sheets, plump the pillows, and fold the towels into awkward triangles like she was auditioning for a spa.

'It's just nice to leave things better than you found them,' she used to say. 'Even if no one notices.'

He'd teased her for it once, calling her the patron saint of tidiness. She'd just smiled and said, 'It's not about tidiness, Tom. It's about kindness.'

That stuck with him. Still did.

Beside him, the coat lay folded; it had felt wrong to leave it slumped. Wrong to treat it like just another piece of clothing. Folding it had felt like an act of respect.

The attic itself had the quiet, cluttered dignity of a space that had seen many temporary occupants: a narrow chest of drawers, the top one refusing to close all the way; a chipped enamel jug, with a single dried hydrangea bloom drooping inside; a framed print of a Dutch windmill, its glass clouded with age; and, in the corner, a stack of magazines from ten years ago.

He tugged gently at the top drawer until it gave with a sigh. Inside, nothing much – a biro without a lid and a single coin, foreign-looking and dulled by time. He turned it over in his palm. An American dime.

IN GOD WE TRUST.

The words caught the light, faint but still legible. He wasn't sure why they made him pause. Maybe because trust had started to feel like something foreign, too – a currency he'd stopped carrying.

He closed his fingers around it, the metal cool against his skin, and slipped it into his pocket. It had no worth here, but the weight of it felt steady. Reassuring.

On the windowsill sat a small pot of brittle soil, the stem of something long dead rising from it. He almost missed it – the faintest curl of green pushing through the dust.

It looked fragile, almost embarrassed by its own persistence. He leaned closer. The shoot was barely more than a whisper of colour, but it was there. Against everything, it looked like it had decided to try again.

He felt something stir at that – a quiet echo of the spring onion, stubborn in its will to survive. Maybe the world wasn't built on grand recoveries but on small, ordinary attempts to keep going.

The attic room hadn't been designed for comfort, yet it

carried the warmth of a place that had been offered rather than sold.

He hadn't slept. Not properly.

He'd always been an overthinker, and sleep had never stood much of a chance. It wasn't just anxiety – he was simply wired that way. Introspective by nature. Emotionally observant. Reflective. An empath, though he rarely called it that. It made him thoughtful, but in times of solitude, that same sensitivity could turn in on itself and spiral. His thoughts didn't simply pass through – they unpacked, rearranged the furniture, and made themselves at home.

And now, in the stillness of Boxing Day morning, his thoughts arrived in their usual stampede.

Clare, first.

He pictured her in the kitchen on Christmas Day. Frantic in the best possible way. The windows steamed up, the smell of rosemary and garlic, and her insisting on cooking potatoes *four* different ways because 'it's Christmas, Tom.' The gravy debate. The ridiculous crocheted party hats. The noise. The warmth.

And the tradition they'd invented by accident in their first year together – making a wreath for the front door, that never quite looked like a wreath, and reindeer-shaped shortbread biscuits for the older people in the flat. She'd pipe little red noses onto them with a level of concentration usually reserved for surgery, and he'd deliver them still warm, knocking on neighbours' doors like it was the most important job in the world.

Then came his own Christmas.

A Pot Noodle. A spring onion. The petrol station with a door chime hanging on for dear life. The teenager with the *Allergic to People* slogan on her T-shirt.

The petrol station already felt like it belonged to another day, maybe even another year. Time didn't run normally there – it stretched and hung in the faint buzz of the drinks fridge. For a moment, he wasn't sure if he'd been in there for minutes or hours.

The road beyond the forecourt had felt emptier than it should have, like the world had been tidied away for the holiday. No lorries. No buses. It was the kind of quiet that didn't invite thought so much as demand it.

And Jackie. First seen as a silhouette in the porch light, with mismatched footwear and hair like it had given up on the day hours ago. She'd looked at him the way you might look at a stray dog you're half-surprised had made it to your door – curious, cautious, but unwilling to turn him away.

He thought about the mountain.

The crunch of snow beneath boots. The silence

that hadn't been empty.

Then Yusuf.

That calm voice. That red bobble hat. That story about footsteps that looked like your own.

He looked at the coat. It hadn't changed, but something about it felt different. Like it had given something away during the night. A secret, perhaps. Or a burden.

Somewhere below the floorboards, a radio crackled into life. He heard a few bars of that same Christmas hymn, soft and distant, as though the house itself was remembering.

Then, just as suddenly, it stopped. Mid-verse.

The silence that followed didn't feel accidental. It lingered, expectant, as though the house itself had paused to breathe.

He exhaled and looked back at the coat. The air seemed to hold something unsaid, the way rooms do after a conversation you weren't meant to overhear.

He reached inside, not really knowing why. Maybe to reassure himself it was still just a coat. Maybe because part of him hoped it wasn't.

His fingers brushed the lining and paused. A sound. The faintest crinkle of paper.

He froze, holding his breath as if the coat might notice. That sound didn't belong to fabric, and the pockets were empty.

He pressed along the seam, and there it was again. Something thin and hidden beneath the stitching.

He traced the edge of the lining with his thumb and found a small tear, no bigger than a coin. It was just wide enough for something to slip through. He eased a finger in and felt the unmistakable texture of card.

He tried to pull it free, but the edge caught on the frayed fabric. He coaxed it gently, inch by inch, until it slid out into the light. A small, cream-coloured card.

He turned it over.

An address.

A number. A street. A Suffolk postcode. And beneath it, in smaller letters, *Please take what I couldn't carry any further.*

It was the kind of message you didn't just read – you absorbed it.

He looked down at the coat again.

He could put it back. Hang it by the door, say nothing, and leave. Let this strange detour end here.

Write it off as exhaustion or grief or the madness of spending Christmas alone.

But his hand was already reaching for his backpack; he wasn't ready for the adventure to end. He lifted the coat with care, put it on, and headed for the stairs.

The stairs creaked beneath him, old wood complaining under each step. The kind of sound that, in another house, might've felt wrong. Here, it just belonged.

Downstairs, the morning was still deciding what it wanted to be. No sign of Jackie. No radio. No kettle boiling. Just the stillness of a place that didn't want to rush anyone. On the kitchen counter, a teapot sat beside a folded crossword. One clue was circled in biro – *Wanderer (6)*. Someone had scribbled a faint *R* beside it, as if they'd started to guess but lost confidence halfway through.

Tom walked through to the lounge. He was greeted by the kind of clutter that told you more about a person than anything else ever could. A giant plastic Egyptian head that looked like it had been rescued from a themed nightclub. A silver mirrored bulldog encrusted in diamantés that caught the light like it was trying to blind anyone who questioned its existence. And a jar of mismatched buttons sat on the mantelpiece beside a ceramic owl with one eye missing. In the corner, a faded postcard from somewhere tropical was tucked into the frame of a mirror, its edges curling.

The low table was a gallery of forgotten things – a chipped teacup filled with pound coins, a half-burnt candle in the shape of Father Christmas, and a knitting project that seemed to have stalled mid-row. The whole room felt like it had been assembled by someone who cared more about stories than matching sets.

He thought about Clare. She always liked things to 'matchy match'. He pictured her standing in a shop once, holding two identical mugs with tiny hedgehogs on them.

'We can't just get one,' she'd said, scandalised. 'It would be chaos.'

She'd arranged their bookshelf by colour, grouped the cushions by tone, and even insisted their toothbrushes coordinate.

'Aesthetic harmony equals emotional harmony,' she used to joke, waving a hand like a designer on a makeover show.

And yet, she'd still happily dog-ear pages. Spill tea on her favourite novels. And leave a half-eaten biscuit on the spine mid-chapter. She liked things neat, but she loved things that felt lived in.

A bookshelf sagged under the weight of paperbacks and dust. Some of the titles were stacked sideways to make room for more: *Ward Seven* wedged between a sun-faded copy of Matt Haig's *The Midnight Library* and a well-thumbed *Reasons to Stay Alive. Five People You Meet in Heaven* sat on top of *One Day*, its cover creased as though it had been opened often. And a thumb-worn *The Boy, the Mole, the Fox and the Horse* leaned against *The Complete Guide to Wildflowers*.

He'd read some and heard of others. One or two stirred memories he couldn't place – long train journeys, damp afternoons in cafés, Clare curled up in the corner of their old sofa with a paperback in one hand and a mug in the other. He let his fingers trail along the row until they paused on the thumb-worn book.

Curious, Tom pulled it free. The spine crackled faintly as he opened it. On the inside cover, in hurried, slightly smudged handwriting, was an inscription:

Keep going. One step, then another.

– A

His breath caught.

A small swallow was scribbled beneath it, the sort of thing you might draw without realising, out of habit.

Between the pages, something fluttered loose and landed in his lap – a narrow strip of photo paper. He picked it up carefully. Four tiny frames, slightly curled with age. Two people crammed into a photo booth, mid-laughter, their heads tipped together. The second frame was blurred, as one of them had clearly moved too soon, and the fourth was overexposed, as if the flash had startled them both.

Behind them, he could just make out the backdrop – a wall painted with steins, pretzels, and a crooked banner that read *Bierhaus Bermondsey* in a looping font. One of those faux-German bars that popped up around Christmas, all bratwurst and bad lighting.

The ink had faded, but the joy hadn't. There was something irrepressible about it – the kind of laughter you couldn't fake, the kind that belonged to people who'd forgotten, just for a second, that life could ever hurt.

He smiled without meaning to. The photo wasn't his, but the moment felt universal. Proof that joy had existed, still existed, somewhere – even if not for him. Not yet.

He slipped the strip gently back between the pages, as though returning it to its rightful place, and turned the book over in his hands again.

Tom stared at the words. There was no mistaking

it – this book hadn't been picked up in a shop on a whim; it had been pressed into someone's hands, the way you do when you're afraid they might not make it through the week without something to hold onto.

Clare used to do that. She never believed in keeping books to herself. If she loved one, it was only a matter of time before she passed it on. She'd have tucked it into someone's coat pocket, slid it across a table with a napkin, or simply handed it over with a hopeful smile.

'I want you to love this too,' she'd say. Like the stories were seeds and sharing them was a way of planting things that might grow later.

Tom ran his thumb over the ink, now faded slightly with time. Whoever had written the inscription hadn't been careless. They'd written quickly, yes, but with intention.

He closed the book gently, almost ceremoniously, as though rough handling might erase the words.

Jackie was nowhere in sight when he stepped out into the hallway. He found a notepad by the phone and tore off a sheet. A pen hung from a chain, and for a moment he just stood there. Writing to a stranger felt strangely more personal than speaking to one. Words on a page couldn't be taken back and couldn't hide behind tone or timing. They'd just sit there, naked, waiting to be read.

He tried to remember the last time he'd written a thank you note. Or the last time he'd properly thanked anyone. He couldn't. He set the nib to the paper and wrote slowly:

Thank you. For the tea. For the coat. For letting me stay.

He paused, pen hovering. Then, as if it had been waiting in him all along, he added:

For not asking too many questions.

He thought of Clare.

She'd been left-handed, always holding the pen like it might try to run away from her. Her handwriting had the tidy confidence of a teacher's – upright, patient, and every letter fully formed. Even her grocery lists looked like classroom chalkboards – perfectly aligned, and every word punctuated like it mattered. She used to underline things twice, add asterisks for reminders, and – without ever explaining why – sometimes end her notes with tiny hashtags.

He could still see one of them, stuck to the fridge under a magnet shaped like a tomato:

Don't forget the bin men tomorrow. And stop buying the cheap coffee. #priorities #domesticbliss

He smiled at the memory, the way her humour always hid in the corners of her precision. The recollection didn't ache – it glowed quietly, as though some part of her still existed in the ink.

The bulb above him flickered just once as he signed his name. It was a soft pulse of light, like the house agreeing. He looked up, half-expecting to hear a sound or to see a shadow, but the glow steadied again, warm and unbothered.

He smiled faintly, unsure whether to thank it too.

Then, he folded the note and tucked it under the edge of the teapot in the kitchen. A quiet farewell.

He turned to go, then noticed the mug Jackie had given him the night before still sitting by the sink with a faint ring of tea at the bottom, catching a sliver of morning light like it wanted to be noticed one last time.

Without really thinking, he filled the basin, rinsed it clean, and set it on the rack to dry. The least he could do. Clare would have done the same. And probably rearranged all the cups while she was at it. She'd have straightened the tea towels, wiped the counter, and left a note with a small heart beside her name. Not because she had to, but because it felt right to leave the world tidier than she found it. The thought made him smile. Not with sadness this time, but with something quieter. Gratitude, maybe. Or the faint relief of remembering how to care.

Outside, the cold hadn't relented, but it didn't sting the same way. The car sat where he'd left it, rimmed with frost, looking as though it had been waiting patiently. He unlocked it, opened the passenger door, and placed the card from the coat on the seat beside him. For a moment, he just looked at it. The line underneath the address:

Please take what I couldn't carry any further.

He didn't know who had written it. Not really. But he was starting to understand what it meant.

He turned the key in the ignition. The engine coughed, then caught.

And without overthinking it – maybe for the first time in months – Tom drove. Toward a cottage in Suffolk, maybe. Or a stranger's unfinished journey. Or just a version of himself he thought he'd lost somewhere along the way.

CHAPTER EIGHT
THE COTTAGE

Tom had never heard of the place written on the card. It wasn't on his satnav, and when he tried it on his phone, the map app spun and sulked as if he'd asked it for directions to a ghost town. The closest it could offer was a vague pin dropped somewhere between two fields, marked only by the word *Coast*.

He drove anyway.

The further he went, the narrower the lanes became. Hedgerows on either side brushed the car. Their branches reached out like curious hands, fingering at the paintwork with the occasional dry scratch. Every so often, the hedges opened just enough to offer a glimpse of blue on the horizon. The sea.

The first glimpse of the sea tugged something loose in him. Clare had loved the coast – the endlessness of it. She'd said it made her feel both small and infinite at once.

He remembered a trip to the Northumberland coast one autumn – a half-planned escape after a week that had gone wrong in every possible way. She'd insisted the cure for everything was 'salt air and a keen walk'.

They'd parked near the dunes at Embleton and followed the curve of the beach toward Dunstanburgh Castle. The wind had been relentless, biting through their coats, but she'd grinned into it like it was daring her to give up.

'It's proof the world doesn't stop just because you can't see what's next,' she'd said, pausing by the water's edge.

The tide had crept toward her boots, and she hadn't moved. He'd laughed and told her she sounded like a fridge magnet. She'd nudged him with her elbow, pretending to be offended, then linked her arm through his.

Later, they'd sat in the car with fogged windows and a paper cone of chips balanced between them, the smell of vinegar and salt thick in the air. She'd drawn a smiley face in the condensation and written *keep going* underneath in her neat handwriting – the same looping script she used for birthday cards and fridge notes.

Before they left the coast, they'd talked about coming back in summer to take the boat out to the Farne Islands to see the puffins. She'd been childishly excited about it and had already looked up the boat times and insisted they'd need waterproof trousers 'because puffins are cute, but they're chaos in feathers'. He'd laughed at that too. He'd promised they'd go. But they never did.

The Farne Islands had been one of many things on their list – a list of places they'd promised to visit together but somehow never got around to. Cornwall. Robin Hood's Bay. Amsterdam at Christmas. The list still sat in a notebook somewhere, half-faded and full of places that now felt like versions of a life that had stopped mid-sentence.

He could still see her reflection in the car window that day – the mustard scarf looped twice around her neck, her grin bright and sure. The memory didn't hurt now. It just rested in him, softened by time, like a tide-smoothed stone.

He looked back to the horizon. He wondered if, somewhere up that same coastline, the wind was still tearing at the dunes and the waves still folding over the same stones. He wondered if she'd ever gone back.

He'd laughed at her words then. Now, they sounded like the kind of thing Yusuf might have said.

The tarmac thinned until it was little more than a single threadbare strip, patched in places with stubborn grass. He passed a cottage with a line of washing snapping in the wind. A pair of socks were knotted together like they'd been fighting in the wash. Further on, there was only the wind, a few crows, and a single fishing boat out on the horizon.

By the time he reached the final bend, the lane had given up on being a road entirely. It dissolved into gravel and sand, dropping him into a place that felt hidden on purpose.

A small cluster of weathered cottages huddled against the wind, their backs to the land and their faces set toward the sea. The nearest one stood slightly apart, looking out over a wide shingle beach that fell sharply to the tide line. The water pushed and pulled at the stones with a sound like a long, slow sigh.

Further along the shoreline, hidden by the curve

of the bay, Tom could just make out a glint of metal – something tall and curved. Seagulls circled overhead, their cries sharp and insistent. Beneath them, the faint smell of smoked fish drifted on the wind from somewhere just out of sight.

He parked on the uneven verge, engine ticking as it cooled. For a moment he just sat there, staring at the cottage in front of him – the one that matched the number on the card. Its walls were an off-white and had been worn smooth by salt and years. The door was painted a pastel green, its brass knocker dulled with age. A small, salt-streaked window looked out over the beach, and a crooked chimney puffed a faint ribbon of smoke into the pale midday sky.

There were no signposts. No plaques. No suggestion this place had ever been marked on a map.

Tom stepped out, gravel crunching under his boots. The wind off the sea slid down the back of his neck and made him pull the coat tighter. He crossed to the front door and hesitated, his hand hovering before he knocked. He'd imagined this moment on the drive over, but now that he was here, he wasn't sure whether to knock. Whether he even wanted an answer.

The door opened before he touched it.

The woman who stood there had hair the colour of

frost, pulled back in a loose knot that seemed to be holding on out of habit rather than design. Her heavy-knit jumper was fraying at one elbow, and there was flour dusted across the front of her apron as though she'd been caught mid-recipe.

'Yes?' she asked, polite but cautious.

'I ... found something,' Tom began, tugging at the coat. 'I think it may have belonged to someone you knew.'

Her gaze dropped to the silver swallow pin still fixed to the lapel. Her breath caught. She didn't speak. She didn't have to. Her eyes filled too quickly for blinking to hide it.

'Where did you—'

'In a hostel near Scafell Pike. Yesterday.'

She stepped aside, opening the door wider, gesturing him in without another word.

The hallway smelt faintly of lemon polish and woodsmoke. A pair of boots stood neatly on a mat by the door. Somewhere deeper in the house, a clock ticked.

She led him down the narrow hall into a small sitting room where a fire crackled quietly in the corner. A low bookshelf sagged under the weight of paperbacks, their spines bleached by the sun.

A log shifted in the fireplace, scattering sparks like small, defiant stars.

On the mantel sat a brass clock that had stopped at 11:22 – the same time Tom's watch had given up on the mountain. The coincidence caught him for a moment and made the hairs on his arms lift.

The hands were frozen mid-tick, but somewhere in the house the ticking rhythm continued – a soft, patient ticking that came and went like a heartbeat behind a wall. It didn't feel eerie, just ... relocated. As though time itself had decided to rest here for a while.

He found the sound oddly comforting. Proof that not everything that stopped was broken – some things just needed somewhere quieter to begin again.

Alice noticed his gaze linger on the mantel but said nothing. The room seemed used to visitors who saw ghosts in small details. She simply gestured to the armchair beside the fire.

She didn't sit immediately – she stood for a moment, her eyes still on the coat, as though half-expecting it to vanish.

'My name's Alice,' she said finally. 'And yes. It was his. Yusuf.'

She lowered herself into a rocking chair, hands resting lightly on her knees.

'I took him in about five years ago. He was a refugee. Came with almost nothing but a rucksack and a tired smile.

'Said he didn't want charity. He just wanted somewhere quiet where he could work and breathe. I don't think he'd slept in a proper bed in months.'

Her voice softened as she looked past Tom toward the window. 'He could be quiet for hours, but it wasn't the sort of quiet that shut you out. You never felt like you had to fill it.

'Sometimes he'd come back from the beach with his pockets full of painted stones and shells, and he'd line the best ones up on the kitchen windowsill.'

She smiled faintly. 'He could cook, too. Simple things, but always thoughtful. Salmon risotto was my favourite.

'Once he insisted on making coffee the way his mother taught him – strong, sweet, and poured into cups so small they made my hands look clumsy. He laughed at that. Proper laughed.'

She paused, her smile faltering. 'There were days when he seemed so tired, like even standing upright was an effort. He never said much, but I sometimes wondered if he carried more weight than anyone should.'

Her gaze returned to the coat. 'That swallow pin? He found it one morning on the beach, half-buried in the shingle. Said it reminded him of home. Not because there were swallows there, but because it meant returning.'

She hesitated. 'He used to stand out on the beach for hours, staring at the horizon. Said he liked the way the tide kept returning, no matter how far it went. But sometimes I thought he was really looking for a way out.'

She paused again, as though weighing whether to go on. 'One of the first weeks he was here, I found him at the kitchen table with the coat spread out in front of him like a patient in need of surgery. He was trying to sew it with fishing line. Said the fishing line was all he had. The needle was bent, and his fingers were shaking from the cold.

I made him tea, took the coat, and stitched it up properly. While I was at it, I slipped my address on a card into the pocket. Told him if the coat ever wandered off – or if he did – it might find its way back here. And if it came back, so could he.'

Tom imagined it as she spoke – the fishing line snagging on the fabric, the bent needle, and the steam curling from a mug of tea. He found himself tracing the seam with his thumb.

'The day he left for Scafell Pike,' Alice continued, 'I told him the weather was turning, but he just smiled. It wasn't the sort of smile that reassured you. It was the kind you wear when you've already made up your mind.'

Her voice thinned slightly. 'When they told me he'd been found without his coat, I knew. He'd given it away. He wouldn't have been able to keep it for himself if someone else was cold.'

The room fell into a shared stillness.

'Would you like to see his room?' Alice asked at last.

Tom hesitated, but she was already on her feet, the faintest tremor in her hands as she led him back into the hallway.

They passed a wall hung with framed photographs. Not of Yusuf, but of the sea in all weathers.

Alice opened the last door on the left.

The air inside was cool and faintly salty. The curtains were half-drawn, letting in a thin light that made everything look paused.

On the bed lay a neatly folded jumper and a rucksack, half-zipped, as if someone had stepped out intending to return. A pair of well-worn boots stood at the foot, laces tucked carefully inside.

On the windowsill sat a single oval pebble, worn

smooth, catching what little light there was. The desk beside it was small, scarred with old scratches. A notebook lay open on its surface, a pencil resting diagonally across the page. Next to it, a mug marked with a tide line of old coffee.

And beside the mug, an envelope.

Cream paper, sealed at the back with a dab of dark red wax. His name was written on the front: *Tom*

He blinked as he rubbed his thumb across the letters as though they might smear, half expecting the ink to lift, the name to fade, and the moment to prove itself imagined.

'It says my name,' he whispered.

Alice stepped closer, her brow furrowing. 'The hand's not easy to read.'

Tom stared again. To him, the letters were perfectly clear. Yet the longer he looked, the more they swam, as if the paper itself wasn't sure.

Alice's voice softened. 'He used to say that what we leave behind has a way of finding the right person. Maybe he meant it as a comfort, but ... I think he believed it.'

She met his eyes, steady but kind. 'If he left this here, then perhaps he wanted it to be found by someone who needed it.'

Tom let the envelope rest in his palm. It felt heavier than paper ought to, as though the weight came from what it might contain rather than what it was.

For a long moment he just stood there, thumb pressed to his name, the room holding its breath around him.

Alice shifted, almost apologetically. 'Would you like me to give you some time?'

He shook his head, though he wasn't sure if he meant it. His fingers curled tighter around the envelope. Whatever was inside had waited this long. Another few minutes wouldn't matter. And yet, the thought of opening it here, in this room that still felt Yusuf's, made his chest tighten.

He slid the envelope into the inside pocket of the coat. It belonged with it, for now.

The fire popped softly in the next room. The sea pressed at the walls with its slow, patient rhythm.

Tom drew a breath, steadying himself, the kind of breath you take before opening a door you can't close again.

He knew he would open it. He just didn't know what it would do to him when he did.

Alice's gaze moved to the windowsill. 'Take the pebble too, if you'd like. He found it on the beach one evening. Said it looked like a heart, though not a perfect one. He kept it here, always within reach.'

Tom hesitated, then picked it up. The stone was cool, its edges smoothed by the sea, its shape lopsided but unmistakable. He slipped it into the pocket beside the letter and gave the room one last look – the bed still neatly made, the notebook open on the desk, the sense of someone who'd just stepped out. Then, he turned and made his way back down the narrow stairs.

The house was quieter now. He paused in the doorway to the sitting room, drawn by the soft warmth of the fireplace. The air in the sitting room felt different now, as though the walls themselves had exhaled.

For a moment, he stood there. Not searching for anything, but just letting the quiet settle.

Then, it came.

A faint sound rose behind him. It was so small, he almost missed it, like a memory deciding whether to return.

The clock on the mantel that had stopped at 11:22 stirred and gave a single, uncertain tick. Then another, the sound barely rising above the crackle of the fire. Not steady yet, but trying, like someone learning how to begin again.

Tom froze, one hand still on the doorframe. He didn't move, didn't breathe, just let it play out – the clock's hesitant return, the faint echo of life in a room that had held its breath for too long. It wasn't magic; it was time remembering itself.

He smiled.

Outside, the wind shifted, rattling the glass in the window, and somewhere beyond the walls, the sea rolled and sighed – a low, steady sound like the tide coming home again.

Behind him, a floorboard creaked softly.

He turned.

Alice was standing in the doorway, her cardigan drawn close, eyes flicking from him to the clock and back again. She didn't speak; she just nodded once, with the faintest smile at the corner of her mouth, as if to say *you heard it too.*

Then she crossed to the fireplace, nudged the fire with the poker, and said gently, 'Funny thing about time. It stops for a bit when someone leaves. But it always finds its way again.'

Tom didn't trust himself to answer. He just nodded, the moment folding quietly between them – something shared and understood but never explained.

He thanked Alice, though the words came out smaller than he meant them to. She smiled – a soft, tired smile that didn't quite hide the ache beneath it – and walked him to the door.

For a moment, they stood together in the threshold, neither seeming in a hurry to end it. The wind pushed at the frame, carrying the scent of salt and something faintly floral from the garden. Alice tugged her cardigan tighter and glanced toward the sea.

'If you ever find yourself this way again,' she said, 'you'll know where to stop.'

He nodded, not trusting his voice.

She reached out, brushed a bit of sand from his sleeve, and let her hand fall.

'Safe travels, Tom.'

He managed a small smile.

'Thank you. For everything.'

Her eyes softened.

'You're welcome, Tom.'

For a heartbeat, neither of them moved. Then she stepped back inside, and he stood on the step, coat collar up against the wind, the smell of woodsmoke clinging faintly to him.

Behind him, the door closed gently – not a slam, just a quiet certainty – leaving only the sea and the road ahead.

Back in the car, the engine silent, he sat with both in his lap – the small, solid pebble, shaped by years of tide, and the fragile envelope, waiting.

He traced the name again with his thumb.

The wind worried at the car, rattling the windows as though urging him on.

He leaned back in the seat and tried to steady himself before breaking the seal.

CHAPTER NINE
THE LETTER

The paper tore with a sound far louder than it should have been. Tom flinched, as if he'd just broken something sacred. The envelope split open, and for a moment he simply stared at the folded sheet inside, afraid of the weight it might carry.

Eventually, he pulled it out and unfolded the page. It resisted at first, then lay flat, waiting.

The handwriting was steady, deliberate, and unmistakably human.

The ink had bled slightly in places, as if written in damp air. There were smudges where a thumb had lingered too long – evidence of hesitation, or care.

Tom's pulse tickled in his throat. He wasn't sure if he was ready for what waited inside the lines.

He began to read:

If you are reading this, then I am gone.

I came here from far away, searching for safety. I found shelter but never belonging.

You can be alive and still feel dead. You can stand in a crowd and still be invisible.

I walked streets where no one knew my name. I spoke, but no one listened. I wanted friends. A hand beside mine on the path. Someone to share the climb. But I had no one. Not in the world, not on the mountain. And the silence became heavier than I could bear.

When the snow comes, it will take me. I will die alone. But I don't want my last act to be only vanishing. If kindness can ripple, let it ripple. I don't want my silence to be the only thing I leave behind.

Do not believe that love dies with those we lose. It changes shape, but it does not vanish. You carry them in memory, in every step you take. I understand this now, too late. Please do not make my mistake. Do not let grief convince you that you walk alone.

If I could not have a companion in life, then let me at least walk beside someone in memory.
I wanted someone to share the journey.
Perhaps now, if you read this, I finally do.
– Yusuf

When the words ran out, Tom let the letter rest on his knees. The paper trembled. Not from the car in the wind, but from him, shaking.

Condensation had blurred the glass, turning the world outside into a watercolour of greys and white.

He read it again. Slowly this time. Line by line. With every sentence, it felt as though Yusuf had reached through time and pressed his thumb into the bruised part of him.

'If you are reading this, then I am gone.'

Gone. Tom mouthed the word. It was such a small word for something so enormous. He knew its weight too well. Gone was the empty side of the bed. The dent in the pillow still shaped to her absence. Gone was her toothbrush in the glass by the sink. Waiting beside his long after there was a reason for it to be there, and yet, sometimes, he swore he could still catch the faint scent of her toothpaste. Gone was the coffee machine she had bought him so he wouldn't waste money every morning at the petrol station down the road. He still used it, but without her the sound it made was just noise, not comfort. Gone were the pots of plants on the doorstep. What had thrived under her fingers now withered.

And gone was the book they had once opened together – *The Top 500 Adventures of a Lifetime.* She had circled pages, promising they'd tick them off one by one. Now it sat closed on a shelf, a catalogue of journeys that would never be theirs.

Clare was gone, and yet every object seemed to insist on her presence by refusing to move. He had been walking in the shadow of that absence ever since.

The silence inside the house began to have a texture it – almost physical. It pressed at his chest when he came home from work, followed him down the hallway, and settled beside him on the sofa. It was strange how absence could sound so loud.

But Yusuf's voice seemed to reach across the silence, telling him that naming loss was not the end of a story but the beginning of a new one. He began to see grief not as an end, but as proof that love had left its mark. A thing to carry with him, not in the same way, but still.

'I came here from far away, searching for safety. I found shelter but never belonging.'

Tom thought of the flat he and Clare had shared. The locks on the doors, the curtains drawn tight, and the routines that looked like stability from the outside. Meals eaten in silence near the end. Walks where their hands no longer reached for each other. And nights when she would laugh at something on her phone, and he would smile without asking, knowing the joke wasn't his to share. He had told himself they were safe together, but it had only been a kind of truce with loneliness. Safety, he realised now, had never been the same as belonging. Safety was rent paid on time, a roof over their heads, and promises muttered half-heartedly to keep the peace. Belonging had been something rarer – the way Clare used to lean against him in a queue for coffee or text him about nothing in particular just to close the distance. Those things had faded long before the end. He had chased the wrong thing, just as Yusuf had – mistaking walls for home, silence for peace, and endurance for love. And in the quiet after Yusuf's words, Tom finally saw the difference.

'You can be alive and still feel dead. You can stand

in a crowd and still be invisible.'

Tom felt the words cut deeper than he wanted them to. The invisibility had crept in quietly, starting with Clare. She stopped mentioning him to friends. Nights out no longer included him. Selfies taken without him in them. Trips and meals they'd once promised to save for each other were now ticked off with other people. The silence when he spoke about how he felt, her eyes drifting past him like he hadn't said a word. Even the small things, like sitting in a café while she scrolled on her phone, her face lit by a glow that wasn't meant for him. He'd sit there, hands curled around a cooling cup, waiting for her to look up and see him again. It was the slowest kind of vanishing – still present, but no longer chosen. Yusuf had given that ache a name, and in doing so, reminded Tom he wasn't the only one who had felt it.

'I walked streets where no one knew my name. I spoke, but no one listened. I wanted friends. A hand beside mine on the path. Someone to share the climb.'

Tom closed his eyes. The climb. The mountain. The sting of cold air in his lungs, the ache in his calves, and the sound of his own breath rising and falling like a metronome he couldn't escape. And over it all, Clare's hand slipping from his in that final argument. It was not just a gesture but a whole history sliding away in a moment. He could still hear the echo of her footsteps retreating down the hallway until there was nothing left but silence and the space she had once filled.

He had wanted her with him for every climb, literal and otherwise. The summits and the stumbles, the breathless scrambles through loose rock, the steady stretches where the ground was kind. He had pictured her beside him at the peaks, sharing the view, laughing at the effort it had taken to get there. But she hadn't been there at the end.

And maybe that was the truth he had refused to face until now – that her leaving was not a detour or a pause. Not something that might be undone with enough waiting or wishing. But the final marker on a path that had never really belonged to them both. She was not meant to finish this climb with him.

'When the snow comes, it will take me. I will die alone. But I don't want my last act to be only vanishing. If kindness can ripple, let it ripple. I don't want my silence to be the only thing I leave behind.'

Tom pressed the heel of his hand into his eyes. Silence. That had been his inheritance too – the silence of the empty house, of messages unsent, of things left unsaid to Clare. But Yusuf's words carried something else.

Not silence. A ripple. A gift. A choice to leave more behind than absence.

Tom's heart ached. He thought about kindness rippling. Clare had lived like that. In the smallest ways, the ways most people never noticed.

He remembered one flight they'd taken, landing on a grey afternoon somewhere over Europe. A pram had been offloaded onto the tarmac, folded and awkward, waiting at the foot of the stairs. A young mother was struggling to put it up, her baby balanced on one arm, the other hand wrestling with the frame that refused to click. Around her, a small crowd of passengers stood in a loose half-circle, watching. Airport staff lingered nearby, staring but not helping.

And then Clare moved. No hesitation, no fuss – she handed Tom her bag and jogged down the steps, hair whipping in the wind, calling out, 'Here, love, I've got it.'

She steadied the baby with one hand and snapped the pram into place with the other, a clean, confident click. The mother laughed, half in relief, half in disbelief. Clare just smiled, brushing the grit from her knees.

Tom had watched from above, embarrassed by how easily she'd done what no one else had thought to. He remembered her saying later, when he'd told her so, 'Sometimes the smallest thing is the biggest thing.'

She'd lived by that. Quiet, instinctive kindness. No audience, no reward – just action.

He remembered the park, when she had spotted a little boy watching the ducks, his dad empty-handed and apologetic. Clare had pressed half their loaf of bread into the boy's hands, grinning as his dad told her he'd never fed ducks before.

And always, always, the hotel beds. She would smooth the sheets and fold them back neatly, even when housekeeping was due. 'One less job for them,' she'd whispered once, eyes twinkling as though she'd revealed a secret. Tiny gestures. Barely noticed at the time. Yet they were Clare. They were her language. Quiet proof that kindness didn't have to be grand to ripple outward.

Yusuf had written the words, but it was Clare who had lived them.

'Do not believe that love dies with those we lose. It changes shape, but it does not vanish. You carry them in memory, in every step you take.'

Tom sighed with the realisation – Clare was in every step of his. In the way he still made the bed the way she liked. And in the memories that arrived without warning. Small things. Invisible things. Acts so ordinary, Tom hadn't realised at the time how much weight they carried. But they were Clare – kindness as instinct and love as an everyday language. Yusuf was right. Love didn't vanish. It simply changed form, tucked into gestures, memories, and habits he could carry forward. Maybe that was the way to keep her close – not by refusing to let go, but by continuing what she had shown him.

She wasn't gone – she had simply changed shape. And maybe that meant he could stop clinging to the ghost of her and start carrying her differently.

He leant back in the seat, eyes burning, and realised the ache in his chest had shifted. It wasn't lighter exactly, but it felt like a wound starting to scar. Tenderness where there had only been rawness before.

'If I could not have a companion in life, then let me at least walk beside someone in memory.'

Tom thought of the storm on the mountain, of Yusuf's steady presence, and of the strange comfort he had felt in the company of a man who was both there and not. Maybe Yusuf had already walked beside him, a companion at last, not in life but in legacy.

'I wanted someone to share the journey. Perhaps now, if you read this, I finally do.'

Tom read that line again and again, the words blurring until they were water on the page. A stranger had found in him what he had been unable to find in himself – someone to share the journey. And in that, Yusuf had given him more than a letter. He had given him permission to go on.

Tom folded the page with reverence, pressing the crease as though sealing a vow.

The wind rattled the car again, but this time it no longer sounded like a warning; it sounded like an urging forward.

He thought of Clare's quiet kindness – the pram on the plane, the bread for the boy in the park, the hotel beds made neat for strangers she'd never meet again. They had seemed like nothing at the time, but now he saw them for what they were – ripples. Proof that the smallest acts could shift the weight of the world, even if only for a moment.

Yusuf had written it. Clare had lived it. And now it was his turn.

The paper sat on his knees, light and fragile, yet heavier than anything he had ever held. He placed it carefully back into the envelope, as if tucking Yusuf into rest at last.

He was not alone. He never had been. Clare was still with him, not as an anchor holding him in place, but as a tide urging him forward. And Yusuf – ghost, guide, companion – had walked him safely down from the mountain so he could see it.

Tom looked through the windscreen. Beyond the glass the world was raw, restless, and alive. Trees bent under the gusts, their branches bowing like they knew the weight of letting go. And for the first time in a long while, Tom felt the faint stirrings of a life that might still be waiting for him – if only he chose to step into it.

He slid the key into the ignition. The engine coughed, stuttered, and then found its rhythm. He tightened his grip on the wheel, the letter safe beside him on the passenger seat, and exhaled. The seatbelt clicked into place, sharp and certain in the quiet.

He looked down at his hands – the same hands that had once held Clare's, that had gripped the rock on the mountain, and that were now holding the steering wheel. The same hands, but not the same man.

'All right,' he whispered, voice breaking but steadying itself. Then, Tom pulled out into the wind.

The car rolled forward, tyres crunching over gravel. Behind him, the cottage grew smaller in the mirror until it was only a pale smudge against the cliffs.

And as he headed for home, the horizon widened – the world quietly made space for him again.

CHAPTER TEN
THE NOTEBOOK

Somewhere, tucked away and undiscovered, lies Yusuf's notebook.

Maybe it waits in a drawer no one opens anymore, or beneath a pile of forgotten things in a stranger's loft, its spine bent and its pages breathing quietly in the dark.

It doesn't tell a story. Not really. Just fragments.

Ink spilled in the fragile space between loss and survival.

Words that were waiting to be found:

I do not know why I write.

Maybe to remember.

Maybe so the world knows she was here.

Her name was Layla.
She laughed with her whole body, like she wanted the walls to feel it too.

The neighbours used to tease that our house sounded like a festival.
Music and the clatter of pots, the air rich with cardamom and soap drifting through the windows.

She hummed when she cooked. Not songs, just sounds, soft and shapeless, like a bird testing the morning.

When she kneaded dough, she talked to it.
'Patience,' she'd say.
'Everything rises in its own time.'

At night, she would leave the light on until I came to bed, pretending she had fallen asleep.
But I always saw the twitch of her smile in the half-dark.

The day she died, she was hanging clothes on the line.
I remember the sound of the pegs clicking

against the basket.
She waved at me.
I waved back.
That is the last clear picture I have.

Then there was shouting. Running.
And the kind of silence that comes only after too much noise.
When I reached her, she was already gone.

The basket had tipped.
A shirt lay twisted in the dust.
One of her scarves broke free and drifted down the street, bright against the grey.
It caught for a moment on a broken fence,
fluttering like a signal I couldn't reach,
then slipped loose and was gone.
The street took it.
My legs would not move.

Later, I found one of her earrings by the step. A small gold hoop, dented, and half-buried in sand.
I kept it in my pocket for months.

Neighbours told me to leave.
Cousins. Strangers.

Anyone still breathing.
They said my name was on a list.
They said the men would come back.

But how could I go?
Leaving her behind felt like killing her twice.

I packed almost nothing: a coat,
a photograph bent at the corner,
a tin of dark chocolate wrapped in foil I would never open,
her earring.
That was all.

On the bus out of the city, I pressed my palms together until they hurt.
Pain was proof. Pain meant I was still here.
But being alive was not the same as living.

The bus was full.
Children cried and were hushed with hands.
An old man clutched a bag like it contained his heartbeat.
A woman whispered prayers into her scarf,
each word a stitch holding her together.

I watched the floor.
Dust swirled with every turn of the wheels.

It reminded me of the dust on Layla's sandals by the door.
She had meant to wash them that afternoon.

The driver cursed.
A dog barked somewhere outside.
We kept moving.

I whispered her name so I wouldn't forget the sound.
Layla. Layla. Layla.
Each repetition smaller, as if memory itself were fading.

At the border, soldiers searched our bags.
One of them found the tin of chocolate and laughed.
'Luxury,' he said, tossing it back to me.
The dent in the lid looked like a thumbprint.
I wanted to tell him it wasn't luxury. It was all I had left of her.
But my throat had already closed.

When the sun fell, the road went black.
Outside, the fields vanished into shadow.
My reflection swam in the glass.
My eyes were hollow, and my face emptied of

the man she'd known.
A ghost looking back at himself.

I closed my eyes and tried to hear her humming,
but the only sound left was the engine,
the crying,
and the low, endless roar
of leaving everything behind.

Sometimes I think the world ended that day.
And I am what was left after it broke.

People tell me I was lucky to escape.
But what kind of luck leaves you breathing when
your reason for breathing is gone?

I write so she doesn't vanish twice:
once from the world,
and once from me.

If someone ever finds this notebook,
and reads her name,
then for a moment she will live again.

That will be enough.

Layla.

CHAPTER ELEVEN
THE SWALLOW

Further into the notebook, the ink had bled in places, forming faint halos where tears – or maybe rain – had touched it.

Some words had become smudges; others clung on, stubborn and clear.

The writing was longer now, the pauses fewer. The handwriting leaned forward, restless and uneven, the ink darker in places where the nib had pressed too hard.

Each sentence slanted slightly downward, as if gravity had already become to claim him.

And then it stopped:

The rain here doesn't stop. And it gets into

everything. The walls, the seams of my coat, and even my bones. It smells different too. And it's not the warm rain I knew at home. Here, it soaks you until you forget what warmth ever felt like. Until you start to believe the damp is a part of you.

The streets are crowded, but I may as well be invisible. People brush past me. No one meets my eyes. I try to speak, but the words never seem to come out.

Neon lights flicker on puddles, colours breaking and reforming under boots. Everyone moves with purpose, heads down, faces lit only by their phones. I tried to catch someone's eye once, but they looked through me like I was made of mist.

One night I ended up under a bus stop, soaked through, shivering, and wondering how long I could keep doing this. The posters behind me had peeled from the glass, faces half-torn and smiles warped by the rain. I thought about closing my eyes and letting the night take me. I even whispered a prayer, though I no longer knew who was listening. Then, I thought of Layla hanging clothes in the sun, her smile as bright as the day itself. The thought of her seeing me like this broke me more than the cold ever could. I kept my eyes open until morning, afraid that if I slept, she would think I had already gone.

And then I met Alice. A woman who looked at me as though I was still a person. She didn't ask questions. She only asked my name, softly, like she wanted to check I was still there. She drove me to the coast. Took me in. Gave me a room. Sheets that smelled of lavender. The faint ticking of a clock somewhere down the hall. The hush of the sea beyond the house. The first night, I woke at every creak, expecting footsteps that never came. By morning, I realised the sound I'd heard was the tide breathing against the shore. For the first time in months, I slept without watching the door.

I didn't trust her at first. I expected her to change her mind, but she didn't. She boiled the kettle. She gave me tea even when I told her I didn't drink tea, setting two mugs down so I wouldn't sit there with nothing in my hands. That simple kindness will never be forgotten. It is strange how the smallest things, like the sound of the spoon against the cup, can feel like a hand steadying your heart.

Her house is quiet, and safe in its way. But safety is not the same as belonging. The walls keep out the wind, but not the ache. Sometimes I think belonging isn't a place at all, but the sound of your name spoken by the right voice. And I don't know if I can belong again. I am grateful, truly, but every night I still lie awake staring at the ceiling, listening to the rain, and the loneliness is louder than anything else. I count the drips on the window frame until I lose track. I think of Layla's voice and try to fit her words to the rhythm, as if I could build her out of sound.

I still wear the coat I brought with me from home. It is heavy now, and the fabric is frayed at the cuffs. The colour has dulled, and it smells faintly of smoke. Of journeys I don't want to remember. Sometimes it feels less like clothing and more like a weight I carry, proof that even here I cannot escape what followed me across the sea. Yet I cannot let it go. It is the only thing left that feels like mine.

This morning, I walked to the shore. The sea was rough. The kind that sounds angry at the sky. The air bit at my face and stung my eyes. I found a small pin half-buried in the sand. It was of a swallow with its wings spread. Layla always said swallows carried souls home. I held it in my hand until the cold hurt. I stared at the horizon, wondering if there was any home left for me at all.

When I returned, I pinned it to the coat. At least for now the coat carries something more than loneliness. A reminder of her.

I have thought about it so many times. How to make the noise stop. How to see her again. I don't want to fade away in the streets, nameless and alone. If I must go, I want it to be somewhere closer to her. Somewhere where the clouds might carry me the rest of the way. Somewhere that feels like the first step toward home.

England's highest mountain.

Tomorrow, I climb.

It was the last thing Yusuf ever wrote. Beneath it, a faint indentation marks where his hand once rested, a pause that never found its ending.

The page itself holds the silence of that moment.

Not finality, but release.

The ink has long since dried, but the intent behind it still lingers, like warmth clinging to a cup after the tea is gone.

You can almost picture him there, sitting at the small desk by the window, the sea just audible through the glass, the pen trembling slightly in his fingers. There is no signature flourish, no farewell – only the quiet certainty of someone who had decided that the next step would not be written in ink.

Somewhere, the notebook waits – in a drawer, or a box, or beneath a pile of forgotten things. And if anyone were ever to find it, they might feel, before they even began to read, that this was not just a record of one man's end, but of the smallest spark of hope that outlived him.

CHAPTER TWELVE
A MAN AND A MOUNTAIN

Yusuf woke before the light.

The room was washed in the dim grey that comes just before dawn – the hour when even the world seems unsure whether to rise. The air had that brittleness that follows a night of rain, and the faint hiss of the sea could be heard through the thin glass of the window.

He sat on the edge of the bed for a while, his breath clouding faintly in the cold. The coat hung from the back of the chair, heavy and waiting. The swallow pin caught the weak light like a patient star. He reached out and ran a thumb over the metal, tracing the curve of its wings. It had tarnished slightly, but the shape still held – defiant and unbroken.

On the bedside table sat the notebook. Its cover was soft with wear, and the corners were bent. The last page remained open, his final words resting in the half-light. For a moment he considered adding one more line – something to soften the ending – but there was nothing left to say.

He turned instead to the letter he had written for Alice, folded neatly beside it. The paper was already creased where he had opened and closed it too many times. He read the first few lines under his breath, then stopped. Reading it again would only make him stay. He set it down, placed the cup he'd used the night before beside it, and smiled faintly at the small ring it had left on the wood.

Downstairs, the cottage was still. The only sound was the soft ticking of the hallway clock. He paused half-way down the stairs, listening for signs of life, but nothing came. The quiet felt like permission.

In the kitchen, the smell of last night's lentil curry hung in the air. His boots stood by the door. He pulled them on slowly, tying the laces with care like a ritual. Beside them sat the lost property basket.

He opened the back door. A thin mist hung over

the garden. He stepped outside, the chill biting at his neck, and glanced once toward the window above. No light yet from Alice's room. He was glad. He didn't want to wake her.

At the fence, he paused. The air was damp, and somewhere nearby a gull called – a thin, mournful sound that drifted toward the sea.

He closed the garden gate behind him with care, the latch clicking softly in the morning fog. The road beyond was narrow and wet, puddles catching the faint blush of dawn. He walked with steady purpose, his boots finding rhythm in the gravel.

The world around him was still half-asleep. Chimneys breathed their first curls of smoke. Curtains remained drawn. A tractor started somewhere far off, its hum carried faintly through the valley.

Yusuf lifted his face to the wind. It was cold, but clean. The kind of cold that clears the mind rather than punishes it. He drew a breath and felt something settle inside him. Not peace, not quite, but resolve.

He thought briefly of Layla. The way she used to hum while hanging laundry. The way she'd said, 'One day we'll live by the sea, and the air will smell of salt instead of smoke.'

She had been right about the sea. Just not about

the living.

The six miles took him close to two hours. When he reached Saxmundham, the first light was spilling across the railway tracks.

He took the early train north, changing four times – Ipswich, then Cambridge, London King's Cross, and finally Euston – each platform colder than the last.

At Ipswich, a young woman tried to wrestle a pram through the ticket gate, her scarf trailing on the wet ground. A stranger helped her, lifting the front wheels clear while others looked on. Yusuf watched from the platform, unseen, the small act catching somewhere deep in him – a flicker of care in a world too hurried to notice. He turned up his collar and waited for the next train, the moment lingering longer than it should have.

At Cambridge, the concourse smelt of coffee. Students with rucksacks spoke in a dozen languages, their laughter spilling across the concourse. It made Yusuf ache for something unnamed. A young man sat nearby on a metal bench, unwrapping a *New Yorker* bagel from its crinkled paper. His red rucksack leaned against his knees, one strap held together with tape. Yusuf watched him take a slow, contented bite, the kind of easy hunger that belonged to people who expected tomorrow to come.

He found a quiet corner beneath the departures board and watched the letters flicker from one destination to another, none of them his.

London was noise and motion. The Underground heaved with people. The air was thick with heat and perfume. At King's Cross, he followed the signs to Euston, moving with the current of strangers who never looked at one another. He bought nothing. Spoke to no one.

On the train north, rain streaked the windows, blurring the fields into watercolour. A girl fell asleep against the glass opposite him, her earphones leaking music too faint to recognise. An elderly man unwrapped a sandwich with trembling hands. Across the aisle strangers sat with their faces lit by their screens, each world sealed inside its own quiet glow. Someone laughed softly at their phone as Yusuf sat with the weight of his coat across his knees.

At Oxenholme, the train emptied. He changed again for the branch line to Windermere – a smaller train, its seats frayed. Between stations, he watched his reflection flicker against the glass.

By the time it reached the end of the line, dusk was

already folding in.

Outside the station, the streets were quiet, shops shuttered, and his footsteps sounded too loud against the emptiness.

Yusuf walked until the road curved upward into open country. When the last of the houses fell away, he stopped and looked back. Behind him, the windows of Windermere glowed like a constellation too far to reach. Ahead was only darkness and the long ribbon of road.

He lifted his thumb at the next pair of headlights. The car slowed, and the puddles splashed softly against the kerb as it stopped beside him. The driver was a man in his sixties, wearing a flat cap and a fleece that smelt faintly of diesel.

'Heading to Wasdale?' Yusuf asked.

The man nodded toward the passenger seat. 'As far as the valley. Hop in before you drown.'

They drove mostly in silence. The wipers beat their steady rhythm as the headlights cut tunnels through the mist.

The man talked a little about the sheep, the price of fuel, and the weather. Yusuf listened, grateful for the sound of another human voice.

When they reached a crossroads where the road forked toward the mountains, the driver pulled over.

'This is me,' he said. 'You'll find a hostel another few miles up. It's rough, but it's dry.'

Yusuf thanked him and stepped out. The car's red lights dwindled into the fog, and the night swallowed the sound of its engine.

He walked the rest of the way, the gravel crunching beneath his boots. When at last he saw the lighted windows of the hostel, he felt something between relief and sorrow.

Inside, the air smelt of pine disinfectant and toast. A woman behind the desk looked up from a crossword and handed him a key without asking many questions. 'Room seven,' she said, her voice kind but tired. Behind her, a pinboard cluttered with faded postcards and photographs of walkers grinning into the wind.

He nodded, thanked her, and climbed the narrow stairs. The carpet was threadbare in the middle, the banister smooth from years of hands. The floorboards creaked beneath his steps.

In his room, he placed the coat across the chair to

dry and sat for a long time without undressing. The radiator ticked faintly. Somewhere down the hall, someone laughed in their sleep.

He lay back and closed his eyes, the sound of the wind threading through the eaves.

Tomorrow, he would climb.

Morning came, and Yusuf adjusted the strap of his rucksack. It was lighter now than it had ever been.

The hostel was quiet when he left. The woman from the desk was gone, though a lamp still burnt faintly in the corner. A plate sat on the counter with two slices of toast cooling beside a small pot of marmalade. He thought, fleetingly, that someone had left it for him, then decided it didn't matter either way.

Outside, the air bit at his face. The road was empty except for a crow picking at something near a ditch. He turned up his collar and began to walk.

He arrived at the car park, and the first hard stones of the trail began beneath his feet.

He paused, taking in the vast, pale rise of the peaks ahead, and then, without another thought, took his first step toward the path.

The mountain was not kind that day. The wind came hard across the ridges, sharp as broken glass, driving into every seam and opening. It flattened the hood of his coat against his head, forcing him to keep his chin tucked into his chest.

The sleet and hail came in waves. The icy pellets stung his cheeks and rattled against his hood like thrown gravel. Ice clung to his eyelashes, turning every blink into a blur.

The storm erased the horizon, reducing the climb to nothing but the next few feet of ground in front of him.

He had no gloves, and his hands were raw with cold, the skin burning at first, then dulling until he could no longer feel anything at all. He kept curling his fingers into fists, willing the blood to return, but they barely seemed part of him anymore.

His legs felt heavy, each step dragging like he was walking in water. But Yusuf kept moving. One step, then another. He told himself the mountain wasn't asking for speed, only persistence.

As the hail rattled against the rocks and the wind roared in his ears, he felt ghosts of the past – Layla's laughter spilling out across a washing line, the warm kitchen light of Alice's cottage, and his coat spread out on the table like a patient in need of mending. Other memories arrived with every gust, uninvited but impossible to turn away.

Still, he climbed.

It was as though his body knew this was not a journey of return.

His rucksack was nearly empty. No food worth mentioning. No map. Nothing that suggested he intended to come down again. All he carried was the coat on his back.

It was the same coat that had crossed the sea with him, its frayed cuffs stiff in the cold. He had once worn it through nights of waiting in ports, through train stations, and through long queues. The swallow pin gleamed. It was a small defiance against the weight it was fastened to.

The path grew harsher as he climbed. Stones shifted beneath his boots, and patches of ice lay hidden, waiting. The mist closed in like a curtain. Cairns rose and vanished in the white, only to reappear when he was almost upon them.

He had not come for a view. He had not come to conquer anything. He had come to give himself to the mountain. And to be closer to her.

The higher he climbed, the more the mountain seemed to test him. The wind screamed through the gullies like voices he almost recognised. Once, when he bent low against a gust, he thought he heard his name carried on the air.

'*Yusuf.*'

He straightened, his heart stumbling, certain for a moment that Layla was there, just out of sight. He turned, but the mist offered nothing back but blur.

He pressed on. His legs trembled, each muscle stiff with cold, but still he forced them forward.

He thought of Layla, her arms lifting sheets from the basket, her laughter filling the garden. He thought of Alice, setting down two mugs of tea so he would not sit empty-handed. Their kindnesses lived in him still, even as the cold pressed harder.

The ground grew steeper. Rocks jutted out from the slope, sharp as blades waiting for a misstep. Yusuf paused, leaning against one, and for a moment he almost gave in. It would be so easy to lie down here, let the snow cover him, and sleep. But he shook his head, forced one more breath, and stepped on.

Then, he saw movement ahead. At first, he thought it a trick of the mist. Maybe a shape conjured by his tiring eyes. But as he got closer, he saw a figure hunched against a cairn.

A man, perhaps forty, cold and tired-looking, with a mop of damp brown hair plastered to his forehead. His cheap nylon jacket was useless against the weather; the zip was broken, flapping open at the chest. His hands were bare, red and stiff with cold. He clutched a paper map that disintegrated in the sleet. A small rucksack sagged at his side, one strap torn.

When he looked up, his eyes widened with something between fear and desperate hope.

'Do you ... do you know the way down?' he stammered. His voice cracked, almost lost in the gale. His teeth chattered so hard the words broke apart. 'I think ... I think I'm lost.'

Yusuf stopped. Despite the mist between them, he could see him clearly. His face was panicked. And his shoulders shook with more than just cold. For a moment, Yusuf saw himself, years younger, standing on another road, in another country, with nothing but fear to hold.

Slowly, Yusuf undid the buttons on his coat. The swallow pin glinted as he pulled it free from his shoulders. Warmth fled immediately, the wind tearing at his shirt.

The young man shook his head, holding up a hand as if to refuse. 'You'll freeze,' he said hoarsely. 'Please keep it.'

But Yusuf only smiled. A weary, faint smile with no argument left in it. He stepped closer, draped the coat around the man's shoulders, and fastened it, ignoring the trembling protest.

'Keep it,' Yusuf said quietly. 'It is yours now.'

Yusuf helped the man to his feet. He was unsteady, and his lips were still blue with cold. He clutched at the map as if paper could anchor him, but his hands shook too violently to hold it flat. Yusuf took it gently from him, folded it, and slipped it into the man's rucksack.

'The path is marked,' Yusuf said, though the mist was too thick to see. He lifted a hand, pointing to where the cairns would lead if the stranger kept his head low and his steps careful.

Together they walked a short way, Yusuf steadying him when he slipped, guiding him from one stone marker to the next. When the man stumbled hard on a patch of ice, Yusuf gripped his arm and hauled him upright with a strength that surprised them both.

'You will make it,' Yusuf told him. 'Follow the stones. Do not stop.'

The man's eyes filled with tears. Whether from the cold or from gratitude, Yusuf couldn't say.

At the next cairn, Yusuf let go of his arm. 'This way will take you down,' he said. 'Keep moving.'

The man nodded, clutching the coat tight around him. He turned to ask Yusuf to come too. But Yusuf was already moving away and back up the mountain. He did not look back.

Yusuf continued as the wind clawed at him, tearing at his shirt where the coat had been, but his steps no longer faltered. He climbed steadily, as if the storm itself had become part of the path. His legs trembled with each movement, yet he carried himself with a strange composure.

The mist thickened until the world was no more than rock and whiteness, but he moved as though he knew the way by heart.

The stranger called after him once, twice, but Yusuf did not turn. His figure rose higher, smaller with each step, until he was little more than a shape against the horizon.

For a moment the clouds broke, just enough for the man below to see him outlined against the ridge, still climbing, still moving higher. His figure rose higher, smaller with each step, until he seemed to belong more to the mountain than to the man watching below.

The slope eased, the ground levelled, and at last the trig point rose from the mist. Solid, immovable, and the one certainty on the summit.

Yusuf rested a hand against the cold stone. For a moment he leaned there, steadying himself, as if greeting the mountain itself.

The storm battered him, but it could not move the quiet that had settled within. He had reached the top of Scafell Pike. Not for victory. Not for a view. But to lay something down.

He lifted his eyes to where the ridge fell away into cloud. There was no fear in him now, only calm, as though every step of his life had led him here.

He drew one long breath and walked on.

His figure moved into the whiteness, toward the edge where the ground dissolved into air.

No one saw him fall. There was no cry. No struggle. There was only a kind of surrender, as if his body had been waiting for permission to rest.

The wind took him first, folding around him with a strange gentleness.

The fall was not violent but slow, like being carried. And, for a moment, he felt weightless. The ache in his chest slipped from him like a coat shrugged off at the door. Even gravity felt softer, as though the mountain itself refused to hurt him.

When he landed, the snow gave beneath him with a sigh.

He lay still.

His breath rose one final time before silence.

Not the silence of absence, but of completion.

The mountain did not judge; it simply accepted.

And then – warmth.

Impossible warmth.

The kind that does not come from fire or blood, but from being *known*.

The warmth of being remembered.

The warmth of being seen.

Layla stood before him, sunlight on her shoulders, her hair moving in a breeze that belonged to no weather he knew. Her smile bloomed, unbroken by time. Behind her, the sea shimmered, and he could hear the faint clink of Alice's kettle and the whisper of water poured into two cups. Every kindness he had ever known seemed gathered there – alive, waiting.

She reached out her hand.

'Come home,' she whispered.

Yusuf's lips parted, but no words came. There was no need. The air itself answered.

He closed his eyes, and the weight – the years, the distance, the ache – slipped quietly away.

The mountain did not mourn or protest; it simply received him. It held what it had been given, folding the snow gently over him as if to keep him from the wind.

By morning, the storm had passed. The ridge lay unmarked but for a faint trail leading upward and ending nowhere. The air was clear. The sun broke through, washing the slopes in a soft, forgiving light.

And far below, in the valley, the river carried the meltwater onwards – quietly, faithfully – toward the sea.

CHAPTER THIRTEEN
THE FIRST POPPADOM

The lights of the Taj Mahal glowed a little too brightly for a place that tried to be cosy, their reflections streaking across the rain-slicked pavement outside.

Inside, the door swung shut with its familiar thud, and warmth and noise hit Tom in the same second. The hum of conversation and the clatter of cutlery against heavy plates, and then there was the smell.

First, the smell of fried onions, ginger, and garlic – what every dish seemed to begin with – made him hungrier than he'd realised. Then, the smell of cumin and coriander seeds, joined by cardamom and cinnamon – the kind of smells that clung to your clothes long after you'd gone home. Somewhere behind it all was the yeasty smell of naan bread baking in the tandoor and the faint smell of fresh coriander drifting from passing dishes – the smell of Boxing Day, year after year.

The smells pulled at something in him – a hundred or more dinners and Friday night takeaways, all from this place. He could still picture the ritual of it all. His dad would always insist on picking up the order himself, claiming it was quicker than delivery. He'd take Tom along, rain or shine, the two of them standing at the counter while order after order rolled out through the open hatch. The waiter would always hand Tom a red and green lollipop while they waited. 'Good lad,' he'd say, nodding solemnly as if this were an act of great im portance. Tom would hold it carefully all the way home, sticky fingers clutching the stick like a medal.

Back at the house, his mum would already have the table set in the dining room – cutlery laid neatly and glasses waiting. She'd unpack the foil containers with ceremony, calling out each dish as she went.

'Chicken madras,' she'd say, tapping the lid. 'One pilau, one plain. And – oh – Bombay potatoes again, surprise surprise.'

His dad would grin. 'You can never have too many.'

Tom would take his seat at the table, watching the steam rise as they dished up together.

Those evenings had their own rhythm of soft chatter, the clink of cutlery, and the warmth that lived between them. Every meal had felt like a small celebration, even when it wasn't meant to be.

And now, years later, the same smell rose to meet him as he stepped inside. A smell that was unchanged, patient, and waiting.

Nothing else had changed either. Not the Christmas tree in the corner, one branch forever bent out of shape. Not the garish gold tinsel they'd been hauling out since the early eighties. And not the staff, who somehow hadn't aged a day and still slipped Tom extra After Eight mints like they did when he was a boy. His dad still complained about the cost of the Bombay potatoes yet always ordered one more portion than was absolutely necessary.

Time had moved everywhere else, but here it had stayed stubbornly still.

His mum was already at the table. So was his dad,

halfway through a Kingfisher and trying to read the menu without his reading glasses, which he'd forgotten. Again.

Tom hesitated in the doorway, suddenly unsure of himself. The thought of sliding back into normality felt almost dishonest, like laughing at the punchline of a joke without catching the start.

Then, his mum looked up. Her face softened instantly.

'There you are,' she said. Not too loud, not too gentle. Just enough.

Tom slid into the booth opposite her. She reached across the table and gave his wrist a squeeze. No fuss. No questions. Just there. She'd done the same when he was little, crossing the road outside school – the same small squeeze that meant, *I've got you*.

There was a fourth place set at the end of the booth. A neatly folded napkin, unused cutlery, and a glass of water already half-filled, catching the light. His mum must have poured it without thinking. Muscle memory, perhaps. She followed his eyes and blinked, realising.

'Oh,' she said softly, almost to herself. 'I must've thought...'

She stopped, gave a small smile, and reached for the glass as if to move it, then left it where it was.

'Never mind,' she murmured, straightening the napkin instead.

Tom didn't say anything. The water rippled faintly as someone brushed past, a small movement that made it look briefly alive.

The space stayed open between them, a quiet acknowledgement of someone who wasn't there, and maybe never would be again.

Then, his dad glanced up from the menu. 'Just in time,' he said, pushing the poppadom basket toward him.

His words carried just enough edge to show he was quietly annoyed that Tom was late.

The poppadoms were stacked unevenly. Tom took one and broke a piece off. He dipped it carefully into the mango chutney, letting the crunch settle between them all like punctuation. His mum took a poppadom too, snapping it so crumbs scattered across the table. She laughed as she tried to scoop up some lime pickle. A bright red blob landed squarely on the front of her top.

'Oh, for goodness sake,' she muttered, dabbing at it with her napkin.

His dad gave a long-suffering sigh and rolled his eyes, though the corner of his mouth betrayed a smile.

Then, his mum glanced up at Tom and said lightly, 'I waited for you! You know the first poppadom's always yours.'

Tom smiled. 'You texted me that,' he said. 'Yesterday.'

Her brow furrowed. 'Did I?'

'Yeah,' he said, nodding. 'Do you not remember? Your message popped up right when I was feeling...'

He stopped himself and shrugged. 'Just ... lost, I suppose. It made me smile.'

His mum chuckled softly. 'You know me! Sentimental after a glass of wine!'

He nodded, still smiling. 'Yeah. But it helped. You didn't know it, but it did.'

Her expression gentled. 'Well,' she said quietly, 'you've always had your share. Even when you weren't here to take it.'

His dad looked up from the menu. 'She means the poppadoms,' he said dryly, 'not the sentiment.'

His mum swatted at him with her napkin, laughing. 'Don't listen to your father. He'll eat every one if you let him.'

Tom laughed, breaking off another piece. The crisp edges shattered between his teeth.

For a moment, the years folded in on themselves. He saw himself as a boy, wedged between his parents in this same booth, tiny fingers covered in crumbs. His mum's hand guiding the basket toward him, whispering, 'Quick, before your dad gets them all.'

He remembered the way she'd wink, the secret little smile that meant, *you're part of this.*

And then the other memory. Colder and lonelier. The dim light of the hostel lamp and the sound of wind pressing against the windowpanes. The message glowing on his phone screen: *The first poppadom's yours.*

He watched her now, carefully stacking the broken pieces into a little pile, her smile steady and unhurried. For a moment, something loosened inside him.

That message – that small, silly sentence about a poppadom – had reached him across the distance when nothing else could. It reminded him that people were still thinking of him and still waiting for him to come back. That message had really said, *come home.*

He hadn't known it then, but maybe that was what pulled him through – not a mountain, not a miracle, but the promise of being back here again, with her hand nudging the basket toward him.

At the next table, a toddler banged a spoon against a plate, demanding rice in a voice too small for such determination. The mother laughed, her bracelets chiming as she tried to keep the spoon still. The father shook his head and failed to look stern.

The toddler's laughter carried across the restaurant – that bright, unfiltered sound only small children have. Tom watched as the waiter appeared with a handful of crayons and a paper placemat, crouching down to the child's height. The little one grinned and immediately drew a lopsided sun, the yellow wax crumbling against the page.

The sight made something in Tom's chest ache and warm all at once. He remembered dropping his first poppadom on the floor here once and crying so hard he'd turned purple. His mum had whispered, 'It's only a poppadom, love,' but he'd been inconsolable. Inconsolable until a waiter, the same one with greying temples who still worked there now, brought him another without a word and gave him a wink.

The memory made him smile. He'd forgotten how many times people had quietly fixed small things for him – things that had felt enormous at the time.

Now, the toddler squealed with delight as a poppadom cracked between tiny hands, scattering crumbs like confetti across the table. The parents laughed, and the sound folded neatly into the restaurant's familiar chorus he'd always known by heart. A clatter of plates, bursts of laughter, and the low murmur of people who'd been coming here for years.

Tom sat back, feeling that same warmth ripple through him – the recognition of simple kindness and of belonging that didn't need explaining.

For a moment, Tom could see himself there with sticky fingers, a curry-stained grin, and his mum pretending to be cross while secretly delighted that he loved the food as much as she did. It struck him that nothing in this room had changed. Only the faces that had grown older around it.

It was ridiculous, Tom thought. Sitting here in a place unchanged by time while everything in his own life had been turned inside out. And yet, that's what made it bearable. Safe.

The waiter hovered with his notepad, eyebrows

raised and pen poised. 'Ready to order?'

'One chicken vindaloo and one chicken madras, please,' Tom's dad said instantly, as though he'd been rehearsing it all the way there. 'One pilau rice and...' He hesitated for a fraction of a second, then added, 'two Bombay potatoes.'

'As long as we don't order three again,' Tom said, sliding in. 'You two never learn.'

'You can never have too many potatoes,' his dad replied.

'Two?' his mum said, pretending to be shocked. 'You always order too many, and you know I'll never eat all mine.'

Tom smiled. He could already picture it. His mum setting down her fork with a satisfied sigh, claiming she was full. After a pause and a not-so-discreet burp, she'd rally and eat a bit more, only to be defeated in the end. The foil tray would come out, as it always did. It would be her lunch the next day.

His dad gave a small shrug, unapologetic. 'Eat what you want and leave what you don't. There is nothing wrong with leftovers.'

The waiter turned to Tom. 'And for you, sir?'

'Paneer jalfrezi,' Tom said, without even glancing at the menu. He never ordered anything else.

'And breads?'

'Chilli naan,' Tom said.

'Peshwari for us,' his mum added quickly. 'One's plenty.'

His dad lifted his hands in mock surrender.

The waiter scribbled the order and disappeared toward the kitchen, leaving them in the glow of a ritual so familiar it was almost a performance – same jokes, same complaints, and always, somehow, one Bombay potato too many.

They didn't ask where he'd been. Or why he hadn't come the day before. His mum just passed him the mint sauce and unfolded her napkin, and his dad tapped the table impatiently as if the food should already be here.

Dinner arrived quickly in steel dishes, still too hot to touch, although Tom's mum still tried with her 'asbestos hands'. The familiar clatter of serving spoons and the steam rising gently from the food were almost part of the family.

Halfway through her vindaloo, his mum reached for a napkin, laughing through a sniffle.

'A good curry always makes your nose run,' she said, with the authority of someone repeating family scripture.

Tom grinned at the memory, his throat catching slightly from the spice and the warmth.

'You say that every single year,' he said.

'Because it's true,' she replied, dabbing at her nose. 'If it doesn't, you've wasted your money.'

His dad reached for his Kingfisher. 'You two are lunatics. Anything hotter than a madras is self-harm.'

'Oh, don't be so dramatic,' his mum said, rolling her eyes. 'You once sent back a jalfrezi for being "too emotional".'

'That's because I like to *taste* my food,' he muttered. 'Not set fire to it.'

Tom laughed, remembering.

'What about that time you dared me to try your vindaloo, Mum?'

She leaned back, triumphant. 'And you did! One bite, and you went bright red. Tears everywhere.'

She'd tried to look sympathetic but couldn't stop laughing.

'That's how you know it's love,' she'd told him, handing over a spoonful of yoghurt. 'It burns a bit, but it's worth it.'

I told your dad, 'Look – he's finally emotionally available.'

Even his dad cracked a smile at that, shaking his head.

'He still finished it, though. Couldn't lose face.'

'Pride before heartburn,' she said cheerfully, reaching for more rice.

Tom laughed again. The heat from the curry rose to his cheeks, his nose beginning to run just like hers. It was ridiculous and perfect. For the first time in a long while, it felt like home wasn't something he'd lost but something that had been waiting for him all along, in the small, ordinary rituals that never changed.

Tom smiled. For a moment, everything was exactly as it had always been.

They talked the way they always did, about the 'bloody pigeons' making a mess of the patio, something his dad had read in his Saga magazine, and about their next cruise, despite his dad swearing blind after the last one that he'd never set foot on a ship again.

Tom listened, ate, smiled, and then, true to form, began to talk. He hadn't meant to, but once he started, it came out in uneven bursts, like a tap that couldn't quite be turned off.

'I went for a climb on Christmas Day,' he said,

pushing his rice around with his fork. 'Scafell Pike. Weather was ... bad. Worse than bad, actually.'

He saw his mum's face crease with worry and rushed to soften it.

'I was fine, though. Mostly. Got a bit stuck near the top, but there was this guy – Muslim fella – who helped me down.'

His mum's eyes widened, bright with wonder.

'An angel, more like. Don't tell me he just appeared out of nowhere?'

Tom hesitated, caught between denial and the urge to spill every strange detail.

'Funny thing, he wasn't even...'

He stopped himself, shook his head, and gave a half-smile instead. 'Something like that.'

His dad shook his head, spearing a piece of chicken. 'Or maybe he was just a bloke out for the climb himself. Christmas Day's probably the quietest time up there.'

But his mum wouldn't let it go. 'No, I believe it. People are sent to us when we need them. You'll never convince me otherwise.'

Tom let them debate, content to sit on the fence. He kept quiet about the missing footprints in the snow, Yusuf's coat, and the drive to the coast. But he told enough. Enough that he sounded like himself again. A part of things rather than apart from them.

Later, as the plates were cleared, his mum reached into her bag.

'Nearly forgot,' she said, handing over a small, flat package. 'Found this in your old room.'

Tom unwrapped the paper.

A packet of spring onion seeds.

He stared at it for a moment, then laughed under his breath.

'How funny,' he said.

His mum tilted her head. 'You all right?'

He nodded. 'Getting there.'

She smiled. 'Thought you might plant them in that little patch out back. Be nice to see something growing again.'

He looked down at the seed packet and smiled. A joke from the universe small enough to fit in his palm.

He turned the packet over in his hands. The paper was soft with age, the corners bent. On the back, in small green print, it read:

Sow between March and July. Keep watered. Harvest once strong enough to stand.

He read the words twice, the instructions catching somewhere between his chest and his throat. It wasn't just about seeds. Not really. It was everything he'd forgotten to do for himself – to be patient and to stand strong again.

He smiled faintly. 'Guess I missed the season.'

His mum reached for her glass, swirling the last of her drink. 'Then plant them anyway. Things come up when they're ready.'

Tom turned the packet over once more, the faint rustle of paper loud in the quiet. It felt like a message, disguised as gardening advice. A reminder that growth isn't about timing – it's about trying again.

He slipped the packet into his jacket pocket.

Tom watched his parents bicker over naan bread, the old rhythm of their teasing looping back into itself like a favourite song. His mum dabbed her nose with another napkin and sighed, half-laughing through the sniffles. His dad topped up his glass, pretending not to smile.

Tom sat back for a moment, spoon idle above his plate, and took it all in – his parents, the steam rising off the dishes, and the familiar Bollywood soundtrack playing faintly through the speakers. Nothing here had changed, not really. But somehow *he* had.

It struck him how much love could hide in the smallest rituals, like a shared poppadom, a running joke, or in the gentle absurdity of watching your mum cry over a curry and call it proof of quality. All the things he used to take for granted had turned out to be the things that tethered him when the rest of the world came loose.

For months, he'd thought healing meant fixing something. Making the past behave. But sitting there, surrounded by spice and laughter and crumbs of poppadoms, he realised maybe it was simpler than that. Maybe it was just this – showing up, eating. Laughing and remembering.

He looked at his mum, her cheeks pink from the heat, and at his dad, pretending to be gruff but still breaking off pieces of naan for her plate. These were the things that had waited for him while he'd been lost – the ordinary miracles that had always been there, patient and unassuming.

When a waiter he hadn't seen before came to clear the table, Tom noticed his accent – maybe Pakistani – soft around the vowels. It caught him off guard.

'Good meal, sir?' the waiter asked, stacking the dishes with practised care.

Tom hesitated, the words sticking for a second before he found them.

'Yeah,' he said quietly. 'Better than I deserved.'

The waiter smiled, not quite understanding but kind enough not to ask. He nodded once and disappeared toward the kitchen.

Tom later watched him weave between tables. Pausing to refill a glass here, to joke with a child there, and moving with the same easy grace Yusuf had shown on the mountain, as though kindness were something that lived in small movements, not in grand gestures.

Tom sat back. For the first time in months, he felt it – that quiet pulse of connection. Something fragile but real. The reminder that the world still held gentle people in it.

When the bill came, Tom patted his pockets theatrically. His dad ignored him as usual and paid for the meal, sliding his card across the table with the briskness of long practice.

Outside, the rain had eased to a drizzle. The street shimmered under yellow lights. The pavement shone like a stage.

The restaurant door swung shut behind them with the usual clatter.

Tom hugged his parents goodbye a little longer than usual.

'Text when you're home,' his mum said.

'I will.'

He sat in the car with the engine idling for a moment. He tucked the seed packet into the glovebox where the spring onion had once sat in its sandwich bag.

It wasn't healing. Not yet. But it was a beginning.

Stillness and motion are two sides of the same breath.

– from the notebook of Yusuf

CHAPTER FOURTEEN
THE PARK BENCH (TOM)

Spring sneaked up on him.

One week, the trees were bare; the next, they were brushed with green, as if someone had painted the park overnight. The light was different too – the kind of light that woke the world without startling it.

The paths were muddy where the frost had receded, and the air smelt faintly of cut grass and damp bark – the scent of things beginning again.

Tom came here more often these days. Not every day, but most. The routine anchored him in a way little else did. It wasn't just the walk or the exercise – it was the pattern. It was the same winding of the path through the trees, the circling of the pond, and the same bench waiting like a punctuation mark at the end of each loop.

That morning he'd watered the onion shoots on his windowsill. Three stubborn green stems had pushed through the soil – survivors from a dozen that never sprouted. He ran a fingertip gently over one of the leaves, surprised by its strength. He still didn't know why he'd planted them. Maybe to prove that something could grow again, even from the smallest thing.

He'd rinsed his mug, leaving it to drip on the rack, and watched a bead of water trace the handle before falling. He stood there longer than he meant to, listening to the faint hum of the fridge and the pipes ticking as the boiler cooled. The sound filled the kind of silence that had once been shared.

The flat felt smaller these days. It was tidy but airless like a waiting room – a place you passed through rather than lived in.

His phone buzzed once.

A message from Mum: *Sunday lunch?*

He let it fade. He wasn't ready to answer.

He locked the door twice without thinking and started down the street, his hands in his pockets.

At the corner, an old man waved him down. He stood beside a lamppost with a folded map clutched in one hand and a walking stick in the other. His coat looked older than he did, and his shoes were caked in dried mud.

'Excuse me, son,' the man said, his voice kind but cracked with age. 'Would you know how to get to St Mark's Church?'

Tom slowed. 'You're close – it's just past the library. Head up the hill and follow the bell tower.'

The man nodded but didn't move right away.

His coat was buttoned wrong, with one fastener out of place, and a leaf clung to the brim of his hat.

Then, the man looked at his map as if it were written in another language. 'Ah yes ... the bell tower,' he murmured. 'I used to hear it every Sunday.'

'You've been before then?' Tom asked.

'Long ago.'

The man folded the map carefully, then looked up and squinted into the pale light.

'Strange morning for remembering, isn't it?'

Tom followed his gaze. A single cloud drifted across the sky. 'I suppose it is.'

The man smiled faintly, as though the sky had said something back.

'You see, sometimes you're sent the long way round,' he said. 'Delays can be ... kind.'

Tom wasn't sure what to say.

'I hope you find it all right.'

'I will,' the man said.

He reached out and squeezed Tom's arm with a gentle, steady pressure that lingered a second longer than it should have.

'You're heading to the park, aren't you? Best not rush it.'

Before Tom could reply, the man had turned away, walking at a pace that seemed both slow and unhurried, as though time itself had bent to meet him.

Tom watched until he was out of sight, his figure swallowed by the bend in the road. Then, he exhaled, glanced once more at the empty pavement, and set off again – later than planned – toward the park, collar turned up against the breeze.

By the time he'd arrived at the park, the sky had turned that uncertain shade between grey and blue.

The park was alive again after months of stillness. Children wobbled on scooters, dogs tugged at leads, and somewhere a radio played faintly from a gardener's van.

The café at the corner had its window propped open, and the smell of chips drifted across the path. A boy sat on the wall dipping one into a paper cup of curry sauce, exactly as Tom used to. The smell pulled him backward in time, and he had to force himself not to stop and buy a portion. The thought of sitting alone on a bench with a greasy cone was suddenly unbearable.

A jogger passed, breath steady and sure, red trainers cutting through the puddles. He caught himself thinking how good it must feel to move that freely.

He adjusted his scarf and followed the curve of the gravel path.

He passed an old man feeding pigeons, crumbs falling like grey snow. A couple argued softly about whether they'd locked the car. Two teenagers sat cross-legged on the grass sharing a packet of crisps, their laughter light and careless. He used to laugh like that once.

When he reached the pond, he slowed. The water mirrored the sky. Ducks sent faint V-shaped ripples across the surface.

He sat on the bench at the edge of the water and sat down, hands deep in his jacket pockets.

The bench was familiar. He'd been here once before – years ago – with Clare.

The park felt too alive for his mood. Laughter carried across the grass, dogs barked, and a toddler chased bubbles that burst just beyond reach. He watched it all from a quiet distance, as if through glass. Lately, he'd felt more like an observer of life than an active participant in it – invisible, sidelined, watching the world move around him but never through him.

He'd been coming here for months now, trying to remember how to exist among people without being able to join in.

A couple walked past the pond holding hands, their steps falling easily in sync. They weren't talking, just moving together in that quiet rhythm people fall into when they know each other's pace. He watched them until they disappeared behind the trees and felt an ache he couldn't quite name – not envy exactly, more the memory of what it felt like to be seen without having to explain yourself.

A child dropped a red mitten near the path. Before Tom could rise, a woman hurried back to scoop it up and tuck it into the child's sleeve. The small, effortless gesture caught him – the way one person could notice another without needing a reason. He felt the ache of it, sharp and brief, like cold air in his lungs.

He turned his gaze back to the pond. The ducks had returned, the same as always, paddling through mirrored clouds. He wondered how many of them were new, how many had survived the winter, and whether it mattered that he couldn't tell the difference.

His thoughts drifted back to that day in the park with Clare. It had ended with rain. They'd run for cover under the bandstand, laughing, clutching a cone of chips between them like treasure.

'We should've brought an umbrella,' he'd said, wiping rain from his face.

'Would've ruined the adventure,' she'd replied.

'You call this an adventure?'

'Best kind.'

He could still smell the vinegar and wet hair and the faint trace of her perfume. He'd wanted to kiss her then but hadn't, and he'd never quite forgiven himself for the hesitation.

He smiled at the memory – almost – then pressed it down.

The present rustled faintly around him: footsteps on gravel, distant chatter, and the rhythmic creak of a pram wheel. Somewhere nearby, faint but distinct, he caught another sound – a steady beat like music leaking from earphones. It grew louder for a moment, then faded.

He looked up in time to see the flash of red again – trainers, fast – rounding the curve of the pond.

Then, a watch beeped – a sharp electronic chirp that broke the birdsong.

'Done,' a voice said, half to herself.

He turned.

It was Clare.

The world contracted to a single heartbeat.

For a moment, he thought of the old man on the street, the one who'd said delays could be kind. Maybe this was what he'd meant – the small pauses that rearrange everything without warning.

She was bent slightly forward, hands on her thighs, catching her breath. Her hair was tied back, a few loose strands sticking to her forehead. Her cheeks were flushed from exertion, but her eyes – those same blue-grey eyes – were bright and alive in a way he hadn't seen in years.

'Tom.'

Her voice caught him like a hook. He said her name before he could stop himself. 'Clare.'

For a moment, neither spoke. The park moved on without them. Ducks bickered; a toddler squealed as bubbles drifted away; and a dog shook itself, sending up a spray of water. The world carried on, and yet, for the two of them, everything seemed to pause.

She straightened slowly. 'Hi.'

'Hi.'

She gestured toward the bench. 'Mind if I...?'

He shook his head. 'No, go on.'

She sat, fiddling with her watch until it beeped again.

Then, she tugged at the cuff of her sleeve, smoothing the same patch of fabric over and over – a habit she'd always had when she was nervous, though he doubted she realised she was doing it.

To him, it felt like the universe had timed her run to end exactly there. It couldn't be chance.

He caught a glimpse of her screen – her smile beside a man he didn't recognise, both of them sunlit and laughing, a medal glinting between them. The sight winded him more than he expected. He tried not to look, but his eyes betrayed him.

She tilted the watch away too quickly, her thumb brushing the screen as if to erase the image. The air between them seemed to shrink, carrying that quiet, embarrassed politeness reserved for things that hurt but can't be acknowledged.

She gave a small laugh. 'If it's not on Strava, it didn't happen.'

'You run now?' he asked, trying for lightness, though it came out more like disbelief.

'Sometimes away from things,' she said, half-smiling.

He chuckled – a short, uncertain sound that didn't quite reach his eyes. Did she mean *him*?

'Anyway,' she said lightly, too lightly, 'I'm a bit addicted to the data.'

Tom nodded, pretending to follow her tone, but something inside him had already quietened – the small, fragile hope he hadn't realised he'd brought with him. He stared out over the pond instead, watching the ripples spread and fade.

They both sat in silence. Ducklings wobbled near the water's edge, tiny specks of down following their mother.

Clare smiled and raised her phone to take a photo. He'd forgotten how she always did that – take photos of the small things, the in-between moments, as though they mattered most.

'They're so cute,' she said.

He managed a faint smile. 'Give it a week and they'll have their own Instagram account.'

That earned him a glance and a laugh. For a heartbeat, it felt almost like before.

But even as they watched the ducklings, his mind filled with darker thoughts like foxes in the night, cold water, and the odds stacked against something so small surviving.

They lapsed again into silence.

After a while, she asked, 'So. How've you been?'

He hesitated. There were dozens of ways to answer and none that felt honest.

'Getting by,' he said finally. 'Some days are better than others.'

She nodded slowly, eyes still on the water. 'That sounds familiar.'

He risked a glance at her. 'And you?'

She took a sip from her flask. 'Running helps. Clears my head.'

'So, you're properly into it then?'

'Completely. Haven't missed a parkrun since January.'

He frowned. 'What's a parkrun?'

Her laugh was light but genuine. 'Seriously? Free 5k runs every Saturday. People just turn up – run, walk, or whatever – and get their times emailed after. You'd love it.'

He raised an eyebrow. 'Love it?'

'You would,' she said firmly. 'I should drag you along sometime. You might surprise yourself.'

He smiled faintly.

They fell quiet again, but this time it wasn't heavy. The air between them felt easier, like a wound that had stopped bleeding even if it hadn't fully healed.

He looked at her properly. She looked stronger and more herself. It was strange – she seemed lighter, as if she'd set something down. He wondered what she saw when she looked at him.

Around her wrist was a thin silver bracelet – the

same one she'd worn that summer in Whitby. He wouldn't have remembered it if it hadn't caught the light in the same way now.

'I should probably say I'm sorry,' he said suddenly.

She turned to him, surprised. 'For what?'

'For ... a lot. For leaning on you so hard. For not seeing what you needed. For trying to fix everything when maybe it wasn't mine to fix.'

She inhaled, then let it out slowly. 'I could have said something sooner. I kept hoping it would get easier if I just carried on. But it didn't.'

He nodded. 'I thought if I held on tight enough, we'd get through anything. Turns out I just squeezed the life out of it.'

Her eyes softened. 'You didn't squeeze the life out of me, Tom. I just ... needed air. I felt like I was always the strong one, and I couldn't keep it up.'

He swallowed. The words hurt, but they were true.

'I never stopped caring,' she added quietly.

He looked away, blinking hard. 'Me neither.'

A duck flapped against the water, scattering droplets across their shoes. They both laughed, grateful for the release.

'Come on,' she said, standing. 'Walk with me?'

He followed, falling into step beside her.

They walked along the path that circled the pond. The trees arched overhead, leaves trembling in the breeze. The world looked unchanged, but everything inside him felt rearranged.

When they reached the gate, she pointed to the pub across the road, where people were already gathered under patio heaters. 'One drink?'

He hesitated, then smiled. 'Why not?'

They found a table near the back, half in sun, half in shade.

'Chai latte,' Clare said to the waiter, 'and an elderflower cordial with soda.'

Tom grinned. 'Double drinks. You haven't changed.'

She laughed. 'Some people like variety.'

When the waiter turned to him, he ordered, 'Oat milk latte. And an Appletiser.'

Clare raised an eyebrow. 'Oh, so now you're in the club?'

'Double-Drinkers Anonymous,' he said.

She burst out laughing, the kind of laugh that

reached her eyes. For a moment, he saw the girl from the chip van again – sunlight on her face, sea salt on her fingers.

Somewhere near the bar, a radio was playing. The music was low enough to blend into the chatter. He couldn't quite catch the tune, just the faint hum of a woman's voice. Clare tilted her head slightly, as if she recognised it.

Beside their table, an umbrella leaned against the wall, dripping steadily onto the floor. Each drop landed with a soft, rhythmic patter. He barely noticed it, but Clare glanced at it oncc or twice, her eyes following the tiny dark circle it left on the tiles.

They talked easily. About her new job at the school, his parents' cruise plans, and the seedlings on his windowsill. Small things, but they mattered.

Halfway through their drinks, she said, 'You should really try running, you know.'

He groaned. 'I get out of breath walking up the stairs.'

'That's where everyone starts. Let me take you to a parkrun. Saturday. No excuses.'

'I'd look ridiculous.'

'You'd look like you were trying,' she said, meeting his eyes.

Something unspoken passed between them – not a rekindling, but a recognition.

When they parted at the park gate, she tucked a strand of hair behind her ear. 'Maybe I'll see you at a parkrun.'

'Maybe.'

He watched her jog away, light on her feet, red trainers flashing between the trees. Her music started up again, faint but distinct this time.

He thought again of the man with the map and his strange kindness.

Not all delays were cruel, he realised. Some held you still just long enough to meet the right moment – or the right person – again.

The ducklings were still on the pond when he turned back. They followed their mother in a neat line, tiny wakes rippling behind them. He thought about how fragile they looked and yet how certain their movement seemed.

Near the gate, an elderly man dropped a small bag

of apples. Tom stooped to help, returning each one carefully to the bag.

'Cheers,' the man said, surprised.

'No bother,' Tom replied, and meant it.

He walked home through soft drizzle, the air metallic with rain.

Back in the flat, he went straight to the window. The shoots were taller now, bending toward the dim light. One leaf had unfurled. It was fragile and translucent but reaching anyway.

He found himself thinking of Clare and wondering, not for the first time, if she'd planted anything too. Something small. Something that asked for patience. Maybe she had, in her own way.

He touched the leaf lightly, the way you might test a pulse.

'Still going,' he said quietly.

Outside, the rain came more certain and washed his window clean.

The park held them in the same frame for only a moment.

Two lives that had once run together, now moving at different speeds.

He sat where the path ended.

She ran where it began.

For a heartbeat, they shared the same air,

the same light,

the same half-forgotten pull toward each other.

CHAPTER FIFTEEN
THE PARK BENCH (CLARE)

Spring had crept in almost without her noticing. One week the branches were bare; the next they were brushed with green. She could smell cut grass from somewhere beyond the park gates and hear the steady thrum of a mower – proof that winter had finally let go.

Her playlist pulsed through her headphones – the same track she always saved for the last kilometre. The beat wasn't loud; it was just enough to keep her pace. *Step, step, breathe. Step, step, breathe.* The repetition steadied her.

She'd promised herself ten kilometres today. Not more, not less – just the loop she knew by heart. From the bus stop to the pond and back to the bench by the water came to exactly ten, if she hit the corners just right. She liked the predictability of it. No guesswork. No surprises.

She liked things she could measure, like pace, distance, and calories burnt. Things that ended cleanly at zeros. It wasn't about perfection; it was about control. Numbers behaved. People didn't.

Running had become her measure of distance, not in metres but in recovery. Every lap pulled her a little further from the version of herself who used to wait – for messages, for apologies, for permission.

Every kilometre was a small contract with herself. *Keep moving, breathe, and don't think too far ahead.*

She liked the solitude of it. She liked the honesty of her own effort. No one watching. No one asking. Just her and the next step.

Still, there were mornings like this when the world felt too awake for her mood – when she ran not toward or away from something, but simply to keep from standing still.

These days she kept most things to herself. Her

colleagues at school knew about the running, the playlists, and the good coffee place near the gates – not the sleepless nights or the half-written messages she never sent. Privacy wasn't protection anymore; it was just what she knew. People mistook her quiet for composure, and she let them.

Words had always felt risky – once spoken, they couldn't be taken back. So, she learnt to hold them and to file them quietly where no one else could reach. Her friends called her calm. What they meant was unreadable.

Her mind wandered briefly to the classroom – the glitter still in the carpet from art week and the shoebox castle collapsing on the windowsill. She'd smiled through every tantrum that week, saving her sighs for the bus ride home.

Then to her mum, sitting by the window of the flat with a blanket and a cryptic crossword book. Some mornings Clare stopped by before work with granola and paracetamol, pretending she wasn't checking whether her mother had eaten. The smell of toast and antiseptic lingered in her clothes long after she left. The worry was constant – quiet, but always there – like background music you couldn't quite turn off.

She passed the park gate, breath visible in the cool air. The gravel had darkened from a light morning shower, and the sunlight broke across it like metal shards. A boy sat on the wall eating chips, dipping them into curry sauce. The smell of vinegar and salt hit her and made her think, absurdly, of rain-soaked laughter and a cone of chips from years ago.

She could almost feel the warmth of the paper cone again, the way the salt had stung a cut on her finger, and the way he'd looked at her and then away.

That day had ended under the bandstand, her hair dripping. She'd shaken the rain from it and caught Tom's eyes. He'd looked like he wanted to kiss her but didn't.

She'd wanted him to. And then the moment passed, as all moments eventually do.

She turned a corner where the path narrowed, and the railings were slick with rain. Ahead, a group of boys were throwing bread to the ducks beneath the sign that begged them not to.

Tom would have tutted, she thought, and smiled despite herself. She didn't mind. At least the ducks were having a feast.

Her watch showed *9.98 km*. Just a few more metres. She lengthened her stride, counting the steps in her head. The song in her ears built toward its crescendo.

Then, her watch beeped: 10.00 kilometres.

Perfect.

She slowed to a walk, letting air flood her lungs.

'Done,' she muttered, bending forward, hands on her thighs.

And when she looked up, she saw him.

Tom.

At first, she thought her mind had conjured him. But there he was. He was sitting exactly where her loop ended with his coat collar turned up and his hands buried in his pockets. The same stillness she remembered. The same gravity that once held her and, later, held her back.

She felt the shock bloom behind her ribs, but on the outside, she stayed composed. Years of classrooms had taught her how to keep her face calm while everything inside rearranged itself.

For a second, she wondered if this was what her morning delay at the traffic lights had been for – the universe's small, inconvenient kindness.

Her first instinct was to check her reflection in the pond – an old reflex she hated. Some part of her still cared how she looked in his eyes, even after all the months she'd spent trying to unlearn it.

She pulled an earbud free, and the world filled with noise again.

'Tom,' she said, before she could stop herself.

He looked up.

'Clare.'

The name landed between them like something fragile placed on a table.

The world kept moving – ducks bickered, bubbles drifted, and a dog shook water onto its owner – but she felt caught outside of it, suspended between steps.

She straightened, tugging at her ponytail.

'Hi.'

'Hi.'

‘Mind if I…?’ She gestured to the bench.

He shook his head. ‘No, go on.’

She sat and tapped her watch to save the run.

Her fingers found the cuff of her sleeve and smoothed the fabric once, twice, again – an old habit that surfaced whenever she felt exposed. She hadn’t realised she still did it until now.

Out of the corner of her eye, she saw him glance at the screen of her watch and catch the photo. Her and Ethan from the running club, his arm around her shoulders, both red-faced from the relay. She turned the screen away quickly. Not because it was what he thought, but because she didn’t want to explain. Not yet.

To break the tension, she laughed softly. ‘If it’s not on Strava, it didn’t happen.’

‘You run now?’ he asked, and she heard the half-teasing disbelief in his voice – the same tone he used to use when she’d try something new without telling him first.

‘Sometimes away from things,’ she said, half-smiling.

He chuckled, like he thought she was joking. She let him. Easier than admitting that some mornings she ran until her thoughts blurred into noise. Until the ache in her legs felt simpler than the one in her chest.

Tom always spoke unfiltered. He was honest to a fault. He just blurted out what he was thinking or feeling, as if the world would understand. She used to envy that ease. Now she measured her words, afraid of saying too much and hearing it echo later.

She started to worry. When she'd said she sometimes ran away from things, she hoped he hadn't thought she meant *him*. She wasn't running from him – just from the chaos of her life.

'Anyway,' she said, forcing a smile. 'I'm a bit addicted to the data.'

She meant it as a joke, but the words came out thin. He nodded, quiet, his face unreadable. She looked away quickly, pretending to watch the ducks. What she really wanted was a moment to breathe without being seen.

Ducklings wobbled near the bank. She smiled and lifted her phone instinctively. Some habits outlasted everything. She still collected small things – sunlight through leaves, half-finished cups of coffee, ducklings – little proofs that life continued.

'They're so cute,' she said.

He smiled faintly. 'Give it a week and they'll have their own Instagram account.'

She laughed, genuinely this time. There it was – that dry humour, the self-protection dressed as wit. She also heard what he didn't say – the worry behind it, the part of him that feared the fox in the night.

Silence settled, lighter now.

'So,' she said finally. 'How've you been?'

He hesitated. 'Getting by. Some days are better than others.'

She nodded. 'That sounds familiar.'

'And you?' he asked, careful not to sound like he wanted too much.

She lifted her Stanley cup and sipped, buying time.

'Running helps,' she said. 'Clears my head.'

It was the truth, though not the whole of it. Running gave her boundaries, rhythm, and something that answered back when nothing else did. Every finish line felt like a conversation with herself.

'So you're properly into it then?'

'Completely. Haven't missed a parkrun yet.'

He frowned. 'What's a parkrun?'

She laughed, shaking her head. 'Seriously? Free 5k runs every Saturday. People just turn up – run, walk, or whatever – and get their times emailed after. You'd love it.'

He raised an eyebrow. 'Love it?'

'You would,' she said firmly. 'I should drag you along sometime. You might surprise yourself.'

He smiled faintly.

Then came the apology. Sudden. Unearned but real.

'For leaning on you so hard,' he said. 'For not seeing when you needed space.'

The honesty in his voice was the same as it had always been when his guard slipped – plain, raw, and painful.

She wanted to reach out.

She wanted to touch his sleeve and to tell him he didn't have to carry it all like a punishment.

But she stayed still. Some kindnesses felt too easily misread.

She breathed in slowly. 'I could have said something sooner,' she admitted. 'I kept hoping it would get easier if I just carried on. But it didn't.'

She looked down at her wrist, at the pale stripe of skin where her watch tan ended.

'You didn't squeeze the life out of me, Tom. I just needed air. I felt like I was always the strong one, and I couldn't keep it up.'

His face – the mix of regret and recognition – almost undid her.

'I never stopped caring,' she said quietly.

A duck flapped against the water, spraying them both, and they laughed. They were startled and grateful for the interruption.

'Come on,' she said, standing, brushing dust from her leggings. 'Walk with me?'

They moved together. Not as before – not touching, not perfectly side by side – but near enough that their shadows sometimes met.

The trees swayed overhead, and somewhere beyond the fence, someone was playing the same song that had been in her earphones. She didn't mention it, but she noticed.

At the gate, she nodded toward the pub garden, busy under its heaters.

'One drink?'

It felt brave to ask.

Inside, she ordered automatically.

'Chai latte and an elderflower cordial with soda.'

Tom grinned.

'Double drinks. You haven't changed.'

She shook her head, smiling.

'Some people like variety.'

When he ordered an oat milk latte and an Appletiser, she raised her eyebrows.

'Oh, so now you're in the club?'

'Double Drinkers Anonymous,' he said, and she laughed – that instinctive laugh that felt like remembering sunlight.

Somewhere near the bar, a radio was playing. The music was low enough to blur into the chatter, but Clare caught the tune immediately. It was the song they'd once said they'd have for their first dance – half a joke, half a secret promise neither of them had made aloud. The opening chords found her like a touch she hadn't expected. She tilted her head slightly, pretending it was only familiar, not significant, and hoped Tom wouldn't notice.

Near their table, an umbrella leaned against the wall, dripping softly. Each drop marked the seconds between what was said and what wasn't.

They talked.

She told him about the chaos at the school – glitter explosions, missing lunchboxes, and the boy who called her Miss Carrot. She gave him the edited version – the funny stories, the safe details. The rest she left unsaid – the late-night marking, the quiet dinners eaten standing up, and the phone calls with her mum that ended too quickly because she didn't want to sound worried.

He told her about his parents' cruise and the seedlings on his windowsill. She could picture it. Him leaning over the tray each morning, patient, hopeful, and counting small green victories.

Halfway through her chai latte she said, 'You should try running, you know.'

He groaned.

'I get out of breath walking up the stairs.'

'That's where everyone starts. Let me take you to a parkrun. Saturday. No excuses.'

'I'd look ridiculous.'

'You'd look like you were trying,' she said, meeting his eyes.

For a moment the quiet between them felt like something alive.

When they finished their drinks, Clare adjusted her watch strap to steady herself before they parted.

'Maybe I'll see you at a parkrun,' she said.

'Maybe,' he answered.

She jogged away before the pause could lengthen. Her legs remembered the rhythm instantly. *Step, step, breathe.* She didn't look back. She never did – it made it easier to pretend she chose the leaving.

By the time she reached the far gate, her breathing had evened out. She slowed, stretching, looking across the pond. The ducklings were further out now, a perfect little line behind their mother. They looked fragile but certain too, like they trusted the water to hold them.

Her watch buzzed: *Cool-down complete.*

She ignored it, slipped her earphones back in, and started running again, the same song picking up exactly where it had paused.

'Still going,' she said to herself.

She thought of the seedlings he'd described, small

and stubborn on his windowsill. Maybe she'd plant something too. To see what might take root.

That night, she opened her phone and typed a message she didn't send:

Good to see you today.

Then, she deleted it.

She scrolled instead – through photos of the park, the ducklings, and a half-blurred shot of sunlight on the pond. For a moment she hovered over one picture – her trainers by the bench, the reflection of the sky breaking across the water. She almost posted it with a caption about spring or new starts but stopped. It sounded too much like hope, and she wasn't ready to name it yet.

In the kitchen, the radio played softly, the late-night presenter's voice gentle and low. Her mug of tea had gone cold beside the sink.

She went to the window and looked out across the dark street. The park lights blinked faintly in the distance, a small constellation on the edge of the city.

For a moment she thought of the bench, of the ducklings, and of Tom. The thought made her smile.

She switched off the radio and stood in the quiet, listening to the hum of the fridge, the ordinary pulse of the flat around her.

Outside, the rain began – soft at first, then certain, tapping against the glass in uneven rhythms. She watched her reflection distort as the drops slid down the window, the light fracturing across her face.

'Still going,' she murmured, almost without meaning to.

Then, she turned off the light and went to bed.

CHAPTER SIXTEEN
THE SEAT TAKEN

Tom had hated tinsel last year.

It had mocked him from every shopfront and bus window. Gaudy. Smug. Glittering with a joy he couldn't share.

This Christmas morning, it looked different.

Tinsel shimmered from pushchairs, was draped over Santa hats, and wound around the railings at the start line. No mockery. No smugness. Just joy.

For once, he didn't feel like an observer on the outside of it all. Not quite.

He and Clare stood shoulder to shoulder in a crowd of people wearing elf leggings, reindeer ears, and high-vis vests.

The cold felt sharper than he'd expected. It was the kind of cold that made Tom's eyes water and his fingers ache even through his gloves. From a volunteer's coat pocket, carols drifted from a tinny Bluetooth speaker, half-lost in laughter, footsteps, and the scrape of trainers on gravel, but determined to sound joyful.

He watched the clusters of runners stretching and laughing, already part of something he wasn't sure he understood. It was the sort of scene that made you doubt your choice to show up until you remembered why you had.

If someone had told him a year ago he'd spend Christmas Day at a parkrun, he'd have laughed.

Yet here he was, lacing his trainers in the cold December air, barcode wristband snug around his wrist.

He rubbed his palms together, not just for warmth, but to steady the small tremor of nerves he hadn't expected.

A volunteer with a megaphone – a high-vis hero, as Clare called them – tried to corral everyone toward the start.

Most ignored him, caught up in hugs, chatter, dogs in antlers, and that strange electricity of anticipation that always lives in the moments before something begins.

Just then, a trio came hurrying across the car park – Ethan, his partner Ian, and Hallie – half-running, half-laughing, clutching Santa hats and a box of mince pies that looked in real danger of hitting the ground.

'Typical,' Clare said, grinning. 'They always arrive with thirty seconds to spare.'

'Tom, this is Ethan,' she added, introducing the man from the photo on her watch – the one Tom had once mistaken for someone she'd been with.

Ethan bent slightly to catch his breath, then straightened with a bright, open smile. 'We made it! Hallie was convinced the satnav was wrong.'

He gestured to the man beside him. 'And this is Ian – my partner, designated driver, and chief cheerleader.'

Ian grinned, hands in his fleece pockets and wearing jeans – proof enough he wasn't planning to run. 'I don't run,' he said before Tom could ask. 'But I clap like a champion.'

Clare laughed. 'You really do. He's practically a full-time marshal.'

Ian held up the box of mince pies. 'I'll take these and grab a coffee,' he said. 'See you lot at the finish.'

'Don't eat them all,' Hallie said without looking up.

Ethan smiled. 'He'll say he's just carb-loading by proxy.'

'Exactly,' Ian said, lifting the box and already backing away with a grin. 'Teamwork, right? You do the miles, I do the mince pies.'

Clare waved after him.

He lifted the box in mock salute and wandered off toward the café.

Hallie gave a brief wave without looking up, her expression unreadable in that way that could be mistaken for disapproval, even when it wasn't. The Santa hat didn't help.

She was busy fastening two watches, tugging off her hoodie, and tightening the straps on a hydration vest that looked far too serious for a 5K.

Tom had only ever seen ultrarunners wear them. Hallie treated hers like armour.

Clare leaned in. 'She wears it at every parkrun.'

Ethan smiled. 'Hallie never travels light. She's the only person I know who brings emergency gels to parkrun.'

That earned a faint smirk from Hallie, which, Tom noticed, was probably as close to affection as she ever got before a run.

He found himself smiling too, quietly taking it all in – the easy teasing, the mismatched energy, and the unspoken closeness between them.

The run director lifted the megaphone, his voice cutting gently through the chatter as the crowd began to settle.

'Welcome to Christmas Day parkrun number one hundred and seventy-three!'

Applause and cheers.

'Any milestones?'

A few hands shot up.

Someone at the back yelled, 'Fifty volunteering credits!' and was rewarded with a round of applause that rippled through the crowd like a slow Mexican wave.

Others called out numbers – fifty, a hundred, two-fifty – each one met with cheers.

Tom clapped along, a beat behind everyone else, unsure what counted as a milestone. He'd noticed a few runners in T-shirts with big numbers on the back – 50, 100, 250 – and guessed it had something to do with how often they came. It struck him as a nice idea – celebrating the effort it took just to keep showing up.

The run director went on, scanning the crowd with a grin. 'Any tourists?'

A few hands shot up – Dublin, Amsterdam, even someone claiming Australia. Cheers and laughter rolled through the crowd.

'Any first-timers?'

Hallie raised a hand and pointed toward Tom. 'This one!' she called out. 'First ever parkrun!'

A cheer went up around them, light-hearted and sincere. Tom felt a flush rise to his cheeks before he could stop it.

Clare grinned. 'Sorry,' she said, laughing. 'It's a thing – they celebrate everything here.'

He nodded, trying not to smile too widely, but couldn't help it. 'I'm starting to see that.'

'Right then,' the run director said, raising the megaphone again. 'Dogs on short leads, children within arm's reach, and please give the volunteers a big thank-you as you go past!'

The runners edged forward, the familiar buzz of anticipation returning as they jostled for space at the start line. Dozens of wrists hovered, thumbs poised above watch buttons. Tom fumbled with his own, pretending to know what he was doing.

'Don't worry,' Clare whispered. 'It's not about time. It's about showing up.'

'Timers ready?' the run director called. 'Three ... two ... one ...'

A collective exhale.

And then they were off, the whole pack surging forward in a cheerful stampede of jingling bells.

A marshal in tinsel-wrapped antlers clapped her hands and shouted, 'Great start, everyone!'

At the first bend, Hallie breezed past, her hydration vest sloshing.

Someone behind called, 'It's 5K, Hallie!'

She waved dismissively. 'It's always an ultra *somewhere!*'

At one corner, Clare jogged backwards for a few strides beside him. 'See? You're one of us now,' she teased, before speeding ahead again.

By halfway, Tom was ready to give up. His legs burnt, his chest heaved, and he couldn't for the life of him see the point in continuing. But then, Clare, who was now some distance in front of him, turned back, face lit with a beaming smile.

'I'm so proud of you, Tom!' she shouted over the thud of feet. Something in him shifted. He couldn't stop. Not after that.

The run was harder than he'd expected, each step slower than the last, but he kept going. He was surprised by how much he wanted to finish, not just drift away unnoticed.

When the finish funnel came into view, lined with tinsel and fairy lights, he felt a surge of something unfamiliar. Joy, maybe. Or belonging.

Clare was waiting just beyond the line, clapping and calling his name.

He crossed, grinning and breathless.

A volunteer handed him a finish token, and another scanned his barcode.

'That's it – you're officially a parkrunner now,' Clare said, giving him a hug.

He wasn't fast. He wasn't graceful. But he was there. Moving forward.

He lingered near the funnel, watching others come through. Some sprinted, some jogged, and others walked, a few steering prams through the funnel. A volunteer shook sleigh bells each time someone finished, the sound mingling with cheers, finish-line chatter, and the steady beep of scanners.

Hallie had already finished and was standing with Clare a few metres away, her hands on her hips and her breath misting in the cold air. Her usual sharp expression had softened, a rare smile tugging at the corner of her mouth as she clapped in the last few runners.

Ethan had finished long before Tom – first in his age group, Clare said proudly – and had already gone to find Ian at the café to 'safeguard' the remaining mince pies.

Tom stayed where he was, half bent, his hands on his knees, and his legs too heavy to trust just yet. He couldn't remember the last time his lungs had burnt, and his chest had felt this alive.

Two women in matching blue tail-walker vests were making their way up the path, still chatting as they collected the final cones. Clare's eyes widened.

'Daisy? Isla? I didn't know you two were tail walking today!'

Daisy waved enthusiastically, a Santa hat slipping sideways as she bounced toward them. 'Surprise! Best volunteer role going – get a run and a volunteer credit!'

Isla smiled, calmer and softer than Daisy, her tinsel-framed glasses slipping a little as she laughed.

'And we've got our Christmas Day achievement,' she added, holding up her phone to show the little badge on her parkrun app.

Clare laughed. 'Of course you have.'

As their laughter died down, Clare turned to Tom.

'Oh – have you met these two? This is Daisy and Isla,' she said. 'I wasn't expecting to see them today. Daisy's been injured.'

Daisy waved a hand dismissively. 'Nothing dramatic – just a dodgy ankle. Tail walking keeps me moving without me doing anything stupid.'

Isla smiled. 'Which mostly means slowing her down and making sure she doesn't "accidentally" sprint the last kilometre.'

Daisy grinned. 'Old habits.'

Tom hadn't met them before, but he liked them instantly. Daisy's energy was still there – bright and alive, even if she wasn't running – and Isla's calm steadiness balanced her, the two of them orbiting each other with the easy rhythm of old friends.

He surprised himself by liking Clare's friends all at once. There was no pretence – just people who ran, laughed, and let him in.

Within minutes, Clare's friends were telling Tom about every parkrun they'd ever done, swapping stories of muddy courses and heroic sprint finishes. Tom found himself smiling, drawn in by the warmth of them all.

When someone mentioned coffee, Clare nodded toward the café. 'Come on, before Ian eats what's left of the mince pies.'

Hallie groaned good-naturedly. 'He'll have left crumbs and excuses.'

'Then we'll just have to buy cake,' Daisy said, linking arms with Isla as they started walking.

Clare fell into step beside Tom. 'We'll grab a quick coffee, then head back to mine,' she said. 'We're all having Christmas dinner at mine, remember. It'll be chaos, but the good kind.'

Tom smiled. 'Can't wait.'

They joined the stream of runners heading toward the café, laughter and the jingle of bells still hanging in the air. It felt like the kind of morning that didn't need to be special to matter.

The café was already steaming up when they arrived. The windows were fogged, gloves were draped over the backs of chairs, and the smell of coffee and cinnamon rolled through the air. A faint trail of mud marked the floor where runners had queued before them.

Ian had claimed a corner table, looking smug and faintly guilty beside a plate that contained suspiciously fewer mince pies than before.

'Taste-testing,' Ian said, brushing crumbs from his fleece. 'You're welcome.'

Hallie pulled off her hat. 'You tested half the tray.'

'Thoroughness,' Ian said.

Ethan nodded toward the plate. 'For the record, I told him to wait until everyone got here.'

Hallie raised an eyebrow.

'And that worked?'

'About forty seconds,' Ian said. 'Personal best.'

Laughter rippled around the table as Isla went to the counter to order coffees for everyone.

When she returned, balancing a tray of mugs and passing them out with quiet precision, the table broke into knowing laughter.

'Double drinks again?' Daisy said, spotting both a coffee and a banana milkshake for Clare.

Clare grinned. 'Don't judge me – it's tradition.'

Hallie shook her head. 'You can't have both caffeine and calcium.'

'I can,' Clare said, picking up the straw. 'And I will.'

Isla smiled as she set down the last cup.

'Every week it's the same order. I've stopped asking questions.'

Tom found himself between Clare and Daisy, wrapping his hands around the mug as soon as Isla set it down, the heat seeping gratefully into his fingers.

He hadn't realised until now how much he'd missed this – belonging to a group, being folded into laughter that wasn't his own but welcomed him all the same.

Ian leaned back, grinning at Clare. 'You still using my Sunday Long Mix? Track seven's timed perfectly for your last kilometre.'

Clare laughed. 'Still the best bit of motivation I've got. Though I did have to cut *your* karaoke version of 'Eye of the Tiger'.

'That's sacrilege,' Ian said, mock-offended. 'That performance got me through lockdown.'

'Got you through lockdown,' Hallie muttered. 'Nearly finished the rest of us off.'

Daisy leaned towards Tom, her voice stage-whispering with amusement. 'He's obsessed with playlists.

Everything in his life has a soundtrack – *Pre-Run Pep Talk, Midweek Melancholy, Breakfast for Champions…*'

'Don't forget *Cool-Down Classics*,' Isla added, smiling. 'Or *Songs to Ignore While Stretching*.'

'I've got seasonal ones now too,' Ian said, proud of himself. '*Festive Shake-Out*, *Twelve Days of Tempo*, *Silent Night Negative Splits…*'

Clare groaned. 'He once made a cool-down playlist for my two-minute post-run stretch. *Two minutes*, Thomas.'

Tom laughed.

'It's a calling,' Ian said, pretending to be wounded. 'I curate experiences, not playlists.'

Ethan leaned back, smirking. 'He also reckons they'll give him an OBE someday – for services to rhythm.'

Hallie, meanwhile, was half-listening, half-scrolling through her phone, flicking between the morning's photos. The light from the screen caught the edge of her face as she edited one, tilting her head critically.

'Got some good shots for Instagram,' she said, almost to herself. 'Though Ethan's sprint-face might need a trigger warning and may break the algorithm.'

Clare laughed. 'Please tell me you're not adding captions as long as your voice notes.'

Daisy turned to Tom, grinning. 'We call them Hallie podcasts.'

Tom raised an eyebrow. 'Podcasts?'

Hallie didn't look up. 'Some of us are just better at expressing ourselves verbally.'

Daisy sipped her coffee, trying not to laugh. 'She once sent me a voice note that had chapters. Actual chapters.'

'That was one time,' Hallie said, finally smiling. 'And it was important. I just ... prefer voice notes to texting.'

Tom laughed, caught between amusement and nerves. But the tension dissolved quickly – these people were easy. They ribbed each other affectionately, knew one another's quirks, and finished each other's jokes.

And somehow, Tom wasn't outside of it; he was folded in before he knew it.

At some point, Clare's watch buzzed. She lifted her wrist to silence it, and the screen lit up with a photo – her and Ethan from the relay race last spring, both covered in mud and smiling, a single medal hanging between them.

Tom glanced at it, then back at her. Clare caught the look and smiled, tilting her wrist so he could see properly.

'That was last April,' she said. 'The relay that turned into a mud bath. Ethan pulled his calf halfway through his leg, so we ended up running the last stretch together, him hobbling, me half-carrying him, his arm around my shoulders. Everyone said we'd be disqualified, but we didn't care. We just wanted to finish.'

She looked at the photo again, her voice softening. 'That picture reminds me why I run. Not for times or medals. For days like that – people, mud, chaos, and sticking it out when it would've been easier to stop.'

Daisy reached for another mince pie. 'And snacks,' she said with a grin. 'Don't forget snacks.'

Clare laughed. 'Obviously snacks.'

Tom smiled, looking around the table – at Hallie finishing her coffee, eyes half on her phone, at Ethan laughing softly at something Clare had said, at Ian already planning his next playlist, at Daisy talking with her hands, and at Isla laughing quietly, trying – and failing – to stop Daisy from gesturing too wildly.

He thought of the finish funnel, the jingling bells, and the warmth of it all.

He'd spent so long thinking Christmas would never feel the same again. And yet here it was – louder, messier, and somehow more real.

He realised, suddenly, that he was no longer living as a ghost of himself, hovering at the edges of other people's joy, but as someone who belonged.

Clare caught the look on his face before he could hide it. She reached across the table and touched his arm, smiling as if she knew exactly what he was thinking.

'Ready to go?' she asked.

He nodded.

Chairs scraped, mugs were gathered, and coats were pulled tight against the cold.

Outside, the air bit fresh and sharp, the last of the morning frost lingering in the shade. The group moved together toward the car park, voices low and content, and drifted toward their cars.

Tom and Clare headed for his. The car looked as it always did – slightly scuffed around the doors, a hint of pine air freshener that had long since given up, and a spare jumper and a battered travel mug in the footwell.

Clare slid into the passenger seat without a word, pulling the seatbelt across her coat as Tom turned the key. The engine caught with its usual grumble, the heater coughing to life. For a moment, the windscreen fogged between them before clearing again.

She glanced over and smiled. 'Home for Christmas dinner, then.'

Tom nodded, the words catching somewhere deep and good. The car pulled forward, wipers sweeping the last of the frost away as the laughter of their friends faded behind them.

They'd all made it to Clare's flat just as the first drops of sleet began to fall. Inside, coats were left steaming by the radiator, shoes were abandoned by the door, damp laces trailing, and the sound of laughter and clattering pans drifted from the kitchen.

Ethan and Ian set the table, bickering amiably over cracker placement. Hallie – still wearing her hydration vest – was already decanting wine into the front pocket.

Daisy groaned, laughing. 'You're not seriously using that?'

'It's insulated,' Hallie said. 'And frankly, festive.'

The kitchen was alive with movement. Clare moved between oven and counter with cheerful precision, calling out for timings and tongs like a general mid-battle.

She'd insisted on four different kinds of potatoes – because it's Christmas – and sure enough, the counter was chaos: roasties, mash, dauphinoise, and champ made with the spring onions Tom had grown on his windowsill.

He felt oddly emotional watching her mash them in with the butter and milk. Something small, something green, had survived.

It was such a tiny thing – a handful of shoots in a windowsill pot – yet somehow it felt like proof that life went on growing, even in unlikely places.

Steam fogged the windows. Someone put on Ian's *Festive Shake-Out* playlist, and a slightly offbeat rendition of 'Fairytale of New York' filled the room. Daisy danced with the wooden spoon, Isla laughed into her tea, and Clare turned from the stove to shoo them all away before the gravy burnt. But as the chorus kicked in, she caught Tom's eye across the room.

For a moment, neither spoke. The noise of the kitchen faded around them – the clatter, the laughter, the hiss of the kettle – and it was just the two of them, remembering that night in the pub when she sang karaoke.

Clare smiled, just a small, knowing curve of her mouth. Tom smiled back. Then, she turned back to the stove before the moment could linger.

By the time they sat down, the table looked spectacular in that imperfect, lived-in way that made it feel like home. The candles leaned slightly, wax pooling unevenly in jam jars. The cutlery didn't match, but the plates were warm from the oven, and everything glowed with that forgiving, golden light that makes ordinary rooms feel like photographs.

Clare had made handwritten place cards for everyone – little folded pieces of recycled paper decorated with tiny holly leaves and doodled stars.

Tom's name sat neatly between Clare's and Daisy's. He traced the ink lightly with his thumb before setting it down again. He couldn't remember the last time someone had written his name just for him. It was such a small gesture, but it landed somewhere deep. For once, he wasn't a guest passing through other people's stories. He was part of one.

By then, the flat had filled completely with warmth and the scent of turkey. Outside, the sleet had turned to snow.

Before Clare dished up dinner, they pulled their crackers. Paper hats went on at odd angles. Daisy's snapped clean in two, and Hallie wore hers upside down on purpose.

Tom froze when he opened his and found, nestled beside the usual bad joke and flimsy keyring, a small silver swallow pin. Delicate, light, and catching the glow of the candles. For a second he couldn't quite breathe.

He slipped it into his palm, closing his fingers around it as though it might disappear if he looked too long. He turned it over once, feeling the cool curve of the metal against his skin. He glanced up to find Clare setting down another dish, her paper crown slipping over one eyebrow. She caught his eye and smiled – just a quick, unspoken thing – and then she was gone again, back to the kitchen.

Dinner blurred into laughter and seconds and thirds. Clare made sure no one's plate stayed empty for more than a minute. Someone suggested pudding, someone else declared defeat, and somehow both things happened anyway – Clare appeared with a flaming Christmas pudding while Daisy tried to hide behind a napkin, protesting she couldn't eat another bite even as she reached for a spoon. Hallie insisted on 'tiny portions' that somehow doubled after the first mouthful. Ian declared that anything involving brandy was a drink, not a dessert.

Tom laughed until his stomach ached, the kind of laughter that leaves you lighter without knowing why. The swallow pin sat safely in his pocket, cool against the warmth of it all.

When the plates were cleared, Ethan brought out a stack of dog-eared quiz sheets. 'Right,' he said, tapping the table like a referee. 'Round One: Strava or Sonata?'

'Please tell me that's not another music one,' Hallie groaned.

'It's a running one,' Ethan said. 'You have to decide if the phrase is a tempo marking or an actual Strava route name.'

'Examples?' Clare asked, eyes narrowing with mock suspicion.

Ethan looked down at his sheet. 'Okay – Adagio Intervals?'

'Running,' Daisy said confidently.

'Wrong. Music,' Ethan said. 'Bach-to-Back Tempo Run?'

Laughter.

'Running,' Ian said. 'Surely.'

'Correct,' Ethan said, deadpan. 'And Fugue in D Minor?'

Hallie rolled her eyes. 'Music. Obviously.'

'Could be either,' Ethan said, smirking.

The table broke into laughter.

Clare pointed her fork. 'You've definitely made half of these up.'

'Artistic licence,' Ethan said, scribbling scores no one trusted.

At one point, Daisy protested that Death Hill was obviously hers, Clare claimed that she'd once run it in sandals, and Isla awarded herself half a point for enthusiasm.

The quiz rolled on through bonus rounds of *Whose PB Is It Anyway?* and *Guess the Gel Flavour*, followed by Hallie's solemn declaration that they had just enough energy left for one final battle.

'UNO Spin,' she said darkly, producing the box like an ancient relic. 'The game that ended two friendships and a civil partnership.'

'Technically one friendship,' Isla corrected, stacking the cards. 'The other recovered.'

'Barely,' Ian muttered, dealing.

It didn't matter who won. Between the laughter and mock outrage, the room kept shedding small, tender moments Tom knew he'd carry:

Clare refilling everyone's glasses before her own;

Ian tucking a stray curl behind Ethan's ear;

Hallie pretending to cheat so Daisy would roll her eyes; and

Isla quietly rescuing a spill before it reached the crackers.

Tom leaned back, watching them all through the gentle blur of candlelight. For the first time in a long while, he felt it completely – the strange, solid peace of being exactly where he was meant to be.

Later, when the others drifted toward the sofa, Tom stayed behind to clear the plates. The kitchen was quieter now, but not silent – laughter and the murmur of voices spilled through from the living room.

Hallie was mid-rant about how parkrun marshals should have medals – 'proper ones, with ribbons and engraving' – while Ethan tried to argue that volunteering *was* the medal. Ian had already half dozed off, slouched in an armchair, the paper hat slipping over his eyes.

Daisy and Isla were finishing the last of the pudding straight from the dish. Clare was still at the table, chin resting on her hand, smiling at it all.

Tom rinsed a plate, the warm water running over his hands. Through the open door came the steady rise and fall of laughter, the soft clink of glasses, and the scrape of a chair. For a long moment he just stood there, letting it wash through him – the simple noise of a life in motion – and felt the steady rhythm of belonging settle in his chest.

He'd spent so long staring at an empty seat.

But now, surrounded by friends, warmth, laughter, and the woman he still loved, Tom felt no ache. He felt no hollow.

Just the quiet fullness of being exactly where he was meant to be.

He wasn't waiting anymore.

At last, he'd taken his seat.

This story can end in two ways.

You may choose the one that feels truest to you or read both and let them coexist.

Every life, after all, holds more than one ending.

EPILOGUE (VERSION I)
THE BOY, THE MOLE, THE FOX AND THE HORSE

Spring had found its way back.

Buds on branches, daffodils leaning toward the light, and fields slowly remembering their colour after winter's hold.

Tom walked through town carrying a paper bag from the bookshop. He hadn't meant to go in; he'd only ducked inside to avoid a sudden shower. But he'd left with a book pressed against his chest like it was more than paper.

The Boy, the Mole, the Fox and the Horse.

He'd seen it before, on a shelf in *The Loft* – the

inside cover inked with an inscription and a swallow drawn by hand. He hadn't known then how it got there. Now he did.

They'd gone back north together a few weeks earlier – Tom, Clare, Daisy, and Hallie – the four of them deciding to take on the Three Peaks. Not to chase records or to prove anything, but because it felt like something worth doing and finishing together.

They'd started with Scafell Pike. Clare had planned everything with the precision of someone who didn't trust the weather, Daisy packed enough snacks for a week, and Hallie announced – somewhere past Preston – that she'd made a playlist, 'scientifically proven to improve hill performance,' with Ian's help, of course.

By the time they'd reached the Lakes, the rain had set in – that determined kind that soaks everything without ever quite turning into a storm. They stopped in Keswick for coffee and warmth; Tom's car heater had finally given up the ghost. That's where Clare mentioned Jackie.

'Tom says she runs a hostel near the mountain,' she'd said. 'Says she remembers him from Christmas.

Thought we might stop in and say hello.'

Jackie had met them at the door and led them inside. The hallway was still lined with old photographs of walkers mid-laughter, summits wrapped in cloud, and thermoses balanced on stones.

'Back again, Tom,' she'd said, ushering them into the living room.

They shed coats and boots by the fire while Jackie poured tea. For a while they spoke about the journey. The drive had been a kind of chaos only friends can manage – Hallie arguing with the satnav, Clare insisting on stopping at a petrol station every fifty miles to ensure the tank remained full, and Daisy trying to use Kendal Mint Cake as actual currency.

'It's legal tender in the mountains,' she'd declared, waving it at a bewildered cashier.

But then Tom noticed the book and pulled it from the shelf, while Jackie was talking about her guests and how they often left small things behind – a glove behind a radiator, a book tucked where someone else might find it, and a coin from somewhere else, left on the windowsill as if it were payment to the light.

'People think they've lost things,' she'd said, stirring her tea. 'But mostly, they're just leaving a bit of themselves behind for the next traveller.'

Jackie nodded toward the book Tom was holding. 'Stories, like kindness, travel too,' she said.

She told him about a man who'd left that very book behind before climbing the mountain. Said he'd been given it by a kind woman once and wanted to pass it on.

Tom felt it then – a certainty that needed no proof – that man had been Yusuf, though Jackie never said his name. Perhaps she didn't know it.

They stayed longer than planned. Jackie insisted on feeding them soup and bread still warm from the oven. When they finally left, the clouds had lifted, and the sun greeted them at the door.

They made their way to the mountain and climbed together, laughing at the mud and taking turns to carry the bag of snacks Daisy swore was essential.

The mountain was the same – sharp-edged, patient, and utterly indifferent to time – but Tom wasn't. There was a steadiness in him now that hadn't been there before, a quiet acceptance of what had come and what had gone.

At the summit, the clouds parted just long enough to see the valley spread below, washed clean and bright. Clare stood beside him, her gloved hand holding his. Daisy whooped something about cake, and Hallie was already tying a spare buff to her walking pole and claiming the summit for Team Pavemental.

It had started as a joke months ago – their unofficial running group, born out of too many cold Sunday miles and not enough common sense. *Because pavements were hard, and so was life,* Hallie had said, *and you'd have to be mental to love either.* The name had stuck, scrawled next to Hallie's parkrun barcode in Sharpie and on the back of one of Daisy's race bibs and blu-tacked to her fridge.

Hallie called for one last photo for Instagram before they all stood together against the wind. Tom closed his eyes for a moment, letting it move around him, feeling the solid weight of stone beneath his boots. It wasn't about conquering anything. It never had been. It was about the climb itself, the company, and the act of showing up.

And somewhere in that stillness, he thought again of the book in *The Loft* – of how it had waited quietly, ready to be found.

Now he had bought his own, though he knew it

wasn't really just his. He wrote inside the cover in a hand more certain than he expected:

Keep going. One step, then another.

– T

He added the smallest swallow he could manage in the corner.

He paused before closing it, thinking of Yusuf's coat and the silver pin that still lived quietly in his bedside drawer. He'd kept it as a reminder of how a stranger had appeared when he needed saving most, and how not all rescuers leave footprints.

Outside, the town was stretching itself awake again. Shopkeepers lifted blinds, the smell of fresh bread drifted from the bakery, and a child, red-faced from the cold, chased bubbles that kept bursting before they reached him. Tom stood watching for a while, the book under his arm, then turned toward the park.

It was the same park he'd unexpectedly seen Clare running. He sat on the same weathered wooden bench, the paint flaking in places but still solid. The pond was alive again with ducks and the first dragonflies of the year.

He sat for a moment before placing the book down on the bench beside him.

He rested his hand on the cover for a moment, not as a goodbye but as a passing on. He imagined Yusuf doing the same somewhere, years ago, setting something down and walking away, trusting that whoever needed it most would find it.

'Ready?'

He looked up to find Clare standing a few steps away, cheeks pink from the breeze, her hair in plaits beneath a red woollen hat. She held two coffees from the van near the gate.

'Nearly,' he said, rising to his feet.

She glanced at the book, then at him. 'Planting another one?'

He smiled. 'Something like that.'

They walked the path together, coffees in hand, following the curve that looped back. Runners passed them in pairs and clusters, their footsteps steady, easy. Clare said something about 'runner's envy' as Tom watched the trail of them disappear into the trees.

Behind them, a breeze lifted the cover of the book, turning it to the page where his message was written.

Long after they'd gone, a young boy wandered

down the same path with his mother. He was kicking a football that kept escaping into the daffodils. When he ran to fetch it, his eye caught on something left behind on the bench.

A book.

He picked it up carefully, glancing at the cover, then turned it over in his hands. His mother called him on, and he tucked it under his arm as they left – another story carried forward.

Above them, a swallow traced the air. Quick. Certain. Homeward.

EPILOGUE (VERSION II) THE FINAL ACCENT

It took the rescue team three days to find him.

The storm had eased by then, though the wind still moved across the mountain as if unwilling to leave. It tugged at the marker poles and rope lines and whistled low through the gullies like something with unfinished business.

Every ridge and hollow looked the same – endless white on white.

Snow creaked beneath their crampons.

They moved slowly, a line of red and orange figures, spaced ten metres apart, against the pale slope – methodical, exhausted, and bound together by rope and habit.

Radios crackled with bursts of static and clipped voices giving grid references that blurred into the wind like ghosts through the air. Every ten minutes someone called his name into the white, but the sound was swallowed almost immediately. Once, an echo came back – low and uncertain – and for a second they thought they'd found him. But it was only their own voices returning from the rocks.

By the third morning, their voices had grown hoarse. Conversation had shrunk to brief, practical exchanges.

Their head-torches cut through the mist like thin spears of gold. Snow hissed against their jackets and crusted in their eyelashes.

When they reached the summit, the air was still – too still, one of them thought, like a room where someone has just left. Then, a shout went up. Short. Certain.

They found him just off the main path, half-buried where the snow had drifted. His rucksack lay a few feet away, torn open by the fall. His face was turned toward the clouds, the skin pale beneath a film of frost. His arms were stretched forward, palms open, as though he'd been reaching for something even as he fell.

Tom had come so close. Not far from the summit

– close enough to see it, if the weather had cleared.

The wind dropped for a heartbeat, as if listening. No one spoke.

The team leader knelt, removed his glove, and touched two fingers gently to Tom's neck out of instinct, though they already knew. Then he reached for his radio.

'Base, Search One. Casualty located. Grid November Yankee 215 074.'

A pause. 'No signs of life.'

They stood for a long moment with their heads bowed.

'Poor bastard,' one of them eventually said quietly. Not unkindly.

They photographed the scene, logged the coordinates, and began to search the ground for personal effects – slow, deliberate movements, gloved hands brushing through the snow.

A stainless-steel flask lay half-buried nearby, its lid off, the snow around it melted to a shallow ring of water. One of the team tilted it slightly, as if expecting warmth to rise from it, but it was frozen solid.

A few feet away, a phone rested face-down in the snow, its screen cracked and its casing dented. The team leader placed it carefully into a small evidence bag, marking the time and grid reference in a waterproof notebook.

Inside his jacket pocket they found a wallet, the leather darkened but intact. The youngest rescuer opened it slowly, glancing at the team leader before he did, as if to ask permission. Inside were a few banknotes, a Post it note that said:

Keep going.

You've got this.

– C x

a driver's licence, and a single photograph of Tom and a woman standing close together on top of a mountain, smiling into the kind of light that belonged to summer. The photo had been folded once, then carefully smoothed out again. The paper was still dry.

The team leader logged the items on the recovery sheet, his voice low but steady as he spoke into the radio for the coroner's record. Then he paused, looking at the picture a moment longer than he meant to. He slipped it back into the wallet, closed it gently, and returned it to Tom's coat pocket.

When the recovery log was completed, they stood back a while, waiting for the helicopter that couldn't yet fly – the wind was still too strong on the ridge. One of the older rescuers crouched beside the stretcher, resting a gloved hand on the canvas.

'We'll get you down soon, mate,' he said quietly.

'You've waited long enough.'

The others didn't reply, but the meaning moved through them like a pulse.

Half an hour later, as they began the descent, the youngest rescuer looked back once toward the summit, now glinting in the morning light. Later, he said it felt as though the whole mountain itself was grieving with them.

The coroner later called it death by misadventure. Others, quietly, said 'heartache'.

The Village Below

In the village below, they spoke of the man who hadn't come down. Of the sudden storm that swallowed the ridge. Of the lights of the search parties moving like slow, red constellations across the slopes at night.

Dogs barked into the wind and radios crackled with call-signs and grid references that meant nothing to those listening from their doorways.

At The Fell Inn, men stood in damp boots by the fire, their voices low. Someone drew a rough map on the back of a coaster, marking gullies already searched. Outside, a dog waited by the door, nose pressed to the glass. Conversations stopped each time the door opened, as if someone might walk in with news.

Locals left flasks of tea at the edge of the car park for the rescue crews, along with notes written on the back of receipts:

Keep looking. Bring him home.

Someone tucked a candle into the snow by his empty car, its flame trembling but unbroken through the night.

The papers ran small stories:

Missing Hiker in Christmas Blizzard

For a few days, his name filled the corners of the news. Then came other headlines about train delays, sales, and the New Year.

Only the photograph stayed the same – a faint outline of a man in borrowed light, each reprint fading until he was gone from both mountain and memory.

The Petrol Station

At the petrol station near the mountain, a teenager in a T-shirt that read *Allergic to People* checked the CCTV when the police came asking.

She'd been on shift that night – a quiet one, with the heater humming, rain ticking gently at the windows, and the yellow light pooling across the forecourt.

She remembered hearing the door chime. Looked up, thinking someone had come in. A man, maybe – drenched, head down, standing by the counter as if deciding what to say. She couldn't recall his face, only that the air had felt different for a moment – colder, somehow.

When she played back the footage, though, there was nothing.

Just her behind the counter, scrolling through her phone while *Gavin and Stacey* played on the TV. The chime sounded faintly in the recording, but the door stayed closed.

She replayed it twice, then smiled to herself. 'Must've imagined it,' she told the officers. They noted it down but didn't press.

Sightings

A lorry driver who passed that morning swore he'd seen movement on the ridge before the weather closed in – a figure walking against the wind, head bowed, coat flapping like a flag.

Days later, a farmer mending a gate said he'd noticed a flash of red against the snow – the sort of colour that doesn't belong up there. A bobble hat, he thought.

He turned to fetch his binoculars, but by the time he looked again, the slope was empty.

When the search teams arrived, they found only tracks that began and ended without reason. The snow had hidden more than it revealed.

Some of the rescuers said they felt watched, though they never found who – or what – was watching.

The Bells

Down in the valley, the church bells had tolled for Christmas mass.

The sound drifted upward, striking the lower slopes before the wind carried it away. Inside the church, families pressed close in their coats, breath clouding in the cold air. Children fidgeted through carols, thinking of presents waiting at home.

Outside, smoke rose from chimneys and folded itself into the sky. The world continued and no one looked up toward the ridge, where a single figure moved unseen through snow.

Clare

In another part of the country, Clare woke suddenly,

heart pounding, sure she'd heard someone call her name.

The house was dark and still, the kind of stillness that feels like it's waiting for something to move.

For a moment she sat upright, certain she heard the faint sound of rain, though the windows were dry.

Then, she felt a cold air drift through the room gentle but unmistakable, like someone had opened a door and stepped inside.

Her phone screen lit the room in a pale blue glow:

02:47

She frowned – not at the time, but at the strange pull of it, as though she'd been meant to wake just then. A number she'd remember without knowing why.

She hadn't heard from Tom in years. Not really. A few old photos buried on her phone, a memory that surfaced sometimes on long runs. She'd thought about writing to him – just a message to say she'd started running, that he'd probably tease her for it, but she'd tell him about how it clears your head. But she never had. There was always tomorrow.

She told herself it was a dream, lay back down, and pulled the covers tight. But even as she closed her eyes, she kept listening, as though the air might speak again.

The Coroner

Weeks later, in an office miles from the hills, a coroner wrote the words *death by misadventure* in neat blue ink. The clock on the wall ticked toward closing time. The air smelled faintly of coffee gone cold.

He didn't know the man whose name was typed at the top of the page, or the woman who'd once loved him, or the path that vanished under snow. He only knew procedure.

He signed his name, dated the form, and reached for the next file.

To him, it was a form completed, a box filled, a day nearly done.

To others, it was the moment a story stopped. A silence that would never quite end – only learn to live among them.

On the mountain, the snow was already melting, but in the homes that waited, winter had only just begun.

The Return

A month after the search, one of the rescuers drove back to the mountain. He parked in the same car park, engine idling for a moment longer than necessary.

The flasks were gone now and the candle long melted. He walked a few paces up the trail until the wind caught his jacket.

For reasons he couldn't explain, he stopped, turned toward the ridge, and whispered, 'We found you.'

Then he nodded once, as if to someone unseen, and went back to the truck.

The Truth of It

Maybe the world that followed was what the mind builds when it can't accept that it's already over.

The papers wrote of a hiker caught in the storm – a watch stopped at *11:22*, a wallet with the photo of a girl tucked inside his wallet. She was smiling into the sun, hair slightly blown across her face, one arm outstretched. Her name wasn't printed anywhere, but those who knew him said it was Clare.

His car remained where he'd left it, a strange spring onion sealed in a sandwich bag in the glove box.

But perhaps the truth is quieter than that – that somewhere on the mountain, between one heartbeat and the next, Tom Briggs simply stopped being lost.

And as the snow fell, the wind lifted, and the foot-prints faded one by one, the world made space for him again.

Mercy

Everything that followed his fall – the hostel that seemed to appear out of nowhere; the drive to Suffolk and Alice's cottage the satnav didn't recognise; the Boxing Day dinner with his parents and that sudden sense of home; the reconciliation with Clare, the parkrun with her friends, and the Christmas morning in her flat where he found belonging – was the mind's last mercy, painting heaven in familiar colours.

Not what was, but what should have been.

Yusuf had once been real – a man who'd gone into the storm and never returned.

Perhaps he came back not as a ghost but as a guide, telling his story through a letter that never truly existed.

A companion for the final stretch.

A kindness the mountain allowed.

They said Tom must have lost his way in the storm. But maybe he didn't lose his way at all. Maybe, for the first time, he'd found it.

When the rescuers reached him, they couldn't explain the coat folded neatly beneath him, or the swallow-shaped pin that caught the weak winter light.

One of them swore he heard a sound – the faintest hum carried on the wind – as if someone were still walking beside him, keeping him company on the climb home.

And somewhere, the wind still hums.

The mountain was never just a mountain, and the storm was never only weather. We all climb with the weight of something unseen, and sometimes the hardest part is recognising when we've already reached the place we were meant to find.

Maybe heaven isn't somewhere else at all. Maybe it's the moment a lost thing finds its place again – in light, in memory, or in the kindness left behind – or in the empty seat at the table.

A NOTE FROM THE AUTHOR

This story began on Christmas Day 2024, when I climbed Scafell Pike.

Like Tom, I set off carrying more heartache than preparation. I hadn't realised what a feat it would be until I was halfway up the mountain – lost, cold, hungry, and suddenly aware of how alone I was. At one point I fell – nothing more than bruised pride in the end – but it left me wondering what might have happened had things gone differently.

There were few people on the mountain that day, but one encounter stayed with me. I briefly walked beside a kind Muslim man, Ali, who shared his biscuits when I'd forgotten to bring food. His quiet generosity, offered so simply in that bleak landscape, became the seed from which this book grew.

At the time of writing, I'm still waiting for my own happy ending, but I wanted to make sure that Tom found his – at least if you stop reading before the second epilogue.

Clare was inspired by someone who dragged me, reluctantly, to my first parkrun – someone who brought joy and quirkiness into my world in ways I'll always be grateful for. She was my partner for a time, but perhaps not my person. From her came many of the details that shaped Clare – the double drinks, the quiet acts of care, the encouragement that made me a runner, and the belief that small kindnesses matter.

The day I climbed Scafell Pike, I had in fact already run Rothay Park parkrun – just to tick off my Christmas Day challenge.

This novel is a work of fiction, but many of the events depicted actually happened in some form. It carries the memory of real people, real places, and the quiet realisation that even in loneliness, we are never truly alone.

– Robert Longhurst

ABOUT THE AUTHOR

Robert Longhurst is a writer, runner, and optometrist based in Essex, UK. His fiction explores connection, loss, and the small, redemptive moments that remind us we're never truly alone. *A Man and a Mountain* is his debut novel. When he's not writing or prescribing eye drops, he can usually be found lacing up for another parkrun, convinced it's research for his next story.

PASS IT ON

If this story has found you, perhaps it was meant to. Like Clare in the book, you might choose to leave it for someone else to discover – on a bench, in a café, on a train, or anywhere a stranger might need a quiet reminder that kindness still travels. You can also share it with a friend who might need a story of hope and second chances. Sometimes, passing a book on is another way of saying, 'keep going'.

#DoubleDrinks

In the story, Clare orders "double drinks" – one for hydration and one for joy. You can join in by buying two drinks – one for yourself and one for someone else. It might be a friend, a stranger, someone sleeping rough, or even just the next person in line. Or you could ask a café to *pay it forward* and leave a drink waiting for whoever needs it most.

It's a small gesture, but one that captures the heart of *A Man and a Mountain* – that kindness travels, and connection begins in the simplest of moments. Together, we can start a small movement.

Share your *#DoubleDrinks* moment on social media.

Printed in Dunstable, United Kingdom

75998649R00170